KS

THE NEST

In 2007, Paul Jennings' book sales surpassed eight million copies. In 1995 he was made a member of the Order of Australia for Services to Literature and in 2001 was awarded the Dromkeen Medal for his significant contribution to the appreciation and development of children's literature. He lives in Warrnambool, Victoria, on twenty-one hectares of coastal land which he is turning into a wildlife refuge by replacing the introduced plants with species that once made up the original native forest.

# the nest

paul jennings



PENGUIN BOOKS

PENGUIN BOOKS

Published by the Penguin Group
Penguin Group (Australia)
250 Camberwell Road, Camberwell, Victoria 3124, Australia
(a division of Pearson Australia Group Pty Ltd)
Penguin Group (USA) Inc.
375 Hudson Street, New York, New York 10014, USA
Penguin Group (Canada)
90 Eglinton Avenue East, Suite 700, Toronto, Canada ON M4P 2Y3
(a division of Pearson Penguin Canada Inc.)
Penguin Books Ltd
80 Strand, London WC2R 0RL England
Penguin Ireland
25 St Stephen's Green, Dublin 2, Ireland
(a division of Penguin Books Ltd)
Penguin Books India Pvt Ltd
11 Community Centre, Panchsheel Park, New Delhi – 110 017, India
Penguin Group (NZ)
67 Apollo Drive, Rosedale, North Shore 0632, New Zealand
(a division of Pearson New Zealand Ltd)
Penguin Books (South Africa) (Pty) Ltd
24 Sturdee Avenue, Rosebank, Johannesburg 2196, South Africa

Penguin Books Ltd, Registered Offices: 80 Strand, London, WC2R 0RL, England

First published by Penguin Books Australia Ltd, 2009

1 3 5 7 9 10 8 6 4 2



Cover and text design by Tony Palmer © Penguin Group (Australia)
Cover photography by David Glick/Getty Images
Bird footprint graphics by The Pepin Press
Small bird graphic by Andrew Joyner

Typeset in 12/21pt Fairfield by Post Pre-Press Group, Brisbane, Queensland
Colour separation by Splitting Image Colour Studio
Printed and bound in Australia by McPherson's Printing Group, Maryborough, Victoria

National Library of Australia
Cataloguing-in-Publication data:

Jennings, Paul, 1943–.
The nest/Paul Jennings.
9780143008002 (pbk.)

A823.3

The verses on pages 40–43, 45 and 205 are from the 1817 ballad, 'The Rime of the Ancient Mariner', by Samuel Taylor Coleridge.
The quote on page vii is taken from *Eros and Pathos: Shades of Love and Suffering*, by Aldo Carotenuto (Inner City Books, Toronto, Canada, 1989).
Every effort has been made to trace the original source of copyright material contained in this book. The publishers would be pleased to hear from copyright holders of any errors or omissions.

penguin.com.au

*To: Julie, Jane, Penny, Deidre, Katie and Ruth;*
*Russell, Arie, Keith, Percy, Gordon and Peter.*
*Thank you all so much.*

Who would choose innocence,
even sanity, over enchantment?

*Aldo Carotenuto*

*My father is still mesmerised by the hand. He's terrified of its accusing silence. He suddenly takes a little backward run like a footballer lining up for a free kick and staggers over the pit. For a second he seems to be walking on air. He disappears into the hole with a scream. The swirling snowflakes follow him like tiny petals thrown into a grave. I stand a numb and frozen mourner at the edge.*

*A choking sound erupts. Is it from him? Or from me? I can no longer tell what's real and what's not and for an eternity there's nothing. But then I hear moaning and the sound of rocks falling. I want to peer into the hole but I can't.*

*I hear my father scrabbling for purchase on the frozen edge of the pit. His head emerges, glistening and wet.*

*'Help me,' he gurgles. 'Please help me.' He sees the icepick. 'No,' he screams. 'No, no, no.'*

# THE NEST

## I

Charlie's on the stage trying to raise money to bring some Somali kids from Melbourne to the snowfields. The whole of Bright Dale Secondary College is here, listening. I'm sitting on the edge of the aisle in the middle of the hall so I can see her as she talks earnestly into the microphone, telling the students how she needs to raise a further six hundred dollars to give these people a holiday. It takes guts getting up on the stage like that because while most of the school appreciates what she's saying, others think it's a bit of a wank. I'm nuts about her.

Charlie switches on her laptop and begins a Power Point presentation. For a moment her tall frame and long dark hair are outlined on the blank screen as she hurries to the back of the stage to pick up her notes. She returns to the lectern and begins to show photo after photo of refugees in crowded camps. She flicks through the images so quickly that I hardly have time to process them. The last one is a shot of children in Africa picking up single grains of rice that have fallen off the back of a United Nations truck. Charlie leaves this image on the screen as she continues her pitch. The picture makes me anxious and I wish she'd turn it off.

Verushka and Ryan are sitting in front of me. They always hang out together and I can see why from his point of view. She's shortish but with a great figure and knows it. She wears her hair pulled back in a ponytail with a fringe that swoops across her forehead, and her sleepy grey eyes give the impression that she's concealing deep and mysterious secrets. When she moves she holds herself erect and glides along slowly as if she's walking just above the ground. I've never known her to hurry. Sometimes I see her staring at me which makes me feel peculiar.

There's only one word for Ryan – stylish. His bleached hair always looks as if he's just walked out of the hairdresser's. His ambition is to be a graphic artist in an advertising company and he's constantly sketching expensive watches and state-of-the-art furniture draped with sexy women. He'll probably end up buying a publicity agency and sacking anyone over twenty years old.

Charlie's going to try and sell Give Them a Hand certificates of various values, which are just bits of paper stating how much you're willing to donate to the cause. Most certificates are worth five or ten dollars but there's one for sale at five hundred dollars – as if anyone would pay that.

'Who'll buy a certificate?' says Charlie putting her lips close to the mike. 'Come on; bring a refugee child to the snow for a holiday.'

There's no response. It's like a house auction where people are too scared to scratch their ears in case they accidentally buy the place. Finally, Jessica Green, the girls' school captain, puts up her hand and calls out, 'Five dollars.'

A smattering of applause follows her words.

'Thanks, that's a good start,' says Charlie as she writes Jessica's name down on her donor's pad. 'Someone else? These kids have gone through hell.'

Verushka is slumped down in her seat with her eyes closed. Ryan looks bored.

'Twenty dollars,' says a voice from the back. It's Bazza, the Social Involvement teacher. There's another smattering of applause. This act is generous of Bazza because the teachers have already passed the hat around in the staffroom and he's kicked in once already.

'Terrific,' says Charlie. 'Who's next?'

'Forty,' calls out Mr Rogers, the school counsellor. There are a few whistles of approval – not so much because forty dollars is a lot of cash but because everyone likes him.

Another hand goes up from someone towards the front. It's hard to see who it is because he's got his head down in a sort of resigned, modest slump.

'Ten bucks,' he says. It's James Telford, the boys' school captain.

'Thanks, James,' says Charlie. 'Anyone else?'

A few people fidget uncomfortably in their seats. No one's going to buy another certificate.

'Okay,' says Charlie. 'Let's show the world how generous we are.' More silence. It goes on and on and on and Charlie starts to wriggle with discomfort.

She looks straight at me. Now it's my turn to shift uncomfortably.

'Robin? How about you?'

I go to speak but my mouth is dry and before I can get a word out Bazza cuts in.

'Come on, Bright Dale. Show you care. Wake up. We need at least another five hundred dollars.'

When she hears the words '*wake up*' Verushka opens her eyes and blinks in an exaggerated way, pretending that she's been sound asleep. Ryan laughs. He nods at the stage and then sticks one finger in his mouth as if he wants to throw up. Verushka sniggers. I lean forward and whisper, 'Give her a break; she's trying to help refugees.'

Verushka turns around, stares at me and knits her eyebrows in a way that says, 'Are you mad?'

The answer is probably 'yes', if what's been happening in my head lately is anything to go by, but I don't answer because I'm still thinking of how I can make an impression on Charlie.

'Listen, everyone,' she says desperately. 'Weren't you looking at the photos? These kids have come from countries ravaged by famine. They'd love to have what we toss in the bin every lunchtime. We've never known hunger. We've always got meat and fruit and cake.'

Poor Charlie is drowning and no one's going to save her. She'll never get five hundred dollars out of this lot. I feel so sorry for her. I have to do something.

'Five hundred dollars,' I yell impulsively.

There's a collective gasp. Everyone turns around to see who's so rich that they can give away that much money. Verushka turns and gives me a 'you must be joking' stare. Even the teachers sitting up the back are wide-eyed. Bazza stands up.

'Are you sure about this, Robin? Maybe you should talk to your father first.'

At this point I'm totally pleased with myself. Charlie will be rapt. I am her major sponsor. I'm flushed with my own boldness.

'No, Bazza. No worries. It's a good cause.'

Bazza throws me a doubtful but kindly nod and sits down while Charlie writes my name in her pad. She's blushing.

'Thanks, Robin,' she says. 'It's very generous. The rest of you are a waste of space.' She snaps closed her notebook and slips off into the wings of the stage.

After a few hours pass my mood changes. I start to worry about what I've done. I can't stop thinking about it. Why did I do it? I must be crazy.

After school Charlie comes up behind me as I shuffle with the others towards the door of the bus waiting to take us on the long trip back up the mountain. She taps me on the shoulder and beckons me to come round the back where no one can see us. 'Come for tea Sunday night,' is all she says. She looks directly into my eyes and lightly kisses me on the cheek. Then she's gone.

I'm stunned. Does this mean that she likes me or was that just a thankyou for the money? The place where she kissed me is warm and heat spreads across my face and flows into my body. A kiss on the cheek from Charlie is worth five hundred bucks.

Even if I haven't got it.

It takes two hours to get all the way to the ski slopes, and the older students who live up there usually put their bags and coats on the seat next to them so they can be alone. The juniors all fart around and make a lot of noise up the back, which is okay for them because they don't have any homework.

The bus always starts off pretty full but as it winds through the countryside it begins to spit passengers out at little farms and settlements along the way. By the time it reaches the forest there are only ten or so left. Three of these get off at the sawmill and the rest of us stay on for the climb to the top.

I sit behind Charlie so I can look at the back of her neck. Occasionally I catch a whiff of the shampoo in her long hair, which today is in one long plait falling down over the back of the seat. My stomach is still wobbling from the little kiss she gave me. I just go into a daydream as the bus churns its way through farmland and eventually passes into the state forest. I hardly notice when we reach the first mounds of dirty snow left over from a fall a couple of weeks ago. The snow is much further down the mountain this year, which means a long season ahead, and lots of tourists. The bus climbs higher and the trees and road become blanketed in white, leaving just two muddy wheel tracks. Finally these disappear into the snow too, and there's nothing but the roadside markers and a flat ribbon of white to lead us home.

The prospect of dinner at Charlie's on Sunday has really stirred me up. Although I've been to her place I've never been inside or met her parents. She's been to my house for a meal, though – if you could call it a meal. I slap the side of my face with my open hand, trying to knock the thought out of my head. Don't think about it, don't think about it! Too late – my high spirits dissolve like salt in water. The whole thing, which happened a couple of months ago, was a disaster from beginning to end. *I* wasn't the one who invited her, my father did. Charlie's printer had run out of toner so she'd dropped by the workshop to ask me to print out some leaflets about a rally she was organising to protest about our troops being in Iraq. Straightaway the old man started up as if he was very interested in what she had to say – probably just wanted to keep in good with her father because he's the ranger.

'Why don't you come to dinner, dear?' he said, peering at her over his glasses. 'You can tell us more about it.'

'Charlie's too busy, Dad,' I said quickly.

'No, I'm not,' she said. 'That'd be nice.'

I wasn't so sure about that but at least I'd be close to her for a whole evening.

So that night Charlie arrived at the front door holding a big bunch of gum leaves and dried bottlebrush branches. Dad made a fuss of looking for a vase that I knew we didn't have, and after pretending it was lost he sent me out to the workshop to find an empty kero tin. When I finally found it I had to clean it up. There was a swallows' nest on the wall and the birds had dropped mud and straw and red hairy stuff all over the tin. I was supposed to have got rid of the nest weeks ago. No time for that now. Who knows what he'd been telling her while I was gone?

After I got back and put the arrangement on the coffee table he sent me into the kitchen to bring out the food. I could hear him showing Charlie around the lounge room.

'These are gold nuggets I found up near Jacob's Mine,' he said. 'Not big, but valuable. I have a nose for gold.' He showed her the jar with a few tiny nuggets rattling around inside. 'And this is the head of a roo I shot ten years ago,' he went on, pointing to the head of a poor old kangaroo which stares down from the wall. 'I'm a good shot and won the national target-shooting trophy four years in a row.'

That was a lie because I knew for a fact that he'd bought the roo's head in a junk shop. Charlie would know big reds live in the desert, not in snow country, and anyway it's against the law to shoot kangaroos up here in the national park. She must have been biting her tongue because she's not one to keep quiet over something like that.

God knows what she was making of our cluttered old lodge. The lounge has two big sofas, one with horsehair bristling out of a couple of rips in the fabric and the other with cheap foam bulging through the worn holes. Under the kangaroo's head is a pair of crossed antique wooden skis and on another wall is a print of a Tahitian woman reclining along the branch of a tree. Next to this are a few framed cuttings from newspapers, including a photo of the former Prime Minister standing with a bunch of people in front of the chairlift company's new resort. One blurred, grinning face in the crowd has a circle drawn around it with the word 'me' scrawled beside it in Dad's handwriting.

As I came in with the food-laden tray he was pointing to the Prime Minister. 'Now there's a great leader, Charlie,' he was saying. 'Understands the working man.'

'What about the working woman?' said Charlie.

'He's a battler,' said Dad, ignoring her question.

All this time the TV had been blaring out with the wrestling. We sat down on the sofas in front of it and began to eat the greasy chicken that he'd sent me to buy from the take-away behind the ski-hire shop. Dad picked up a chicken leg and sucked loudly, absolutely refusing to see my 'stop it' looks. Charlie must have known what I was feeling because the next minute she was picking up her own chicken leg and making slurping noises too. She did it in this sort of delicate way and I knew she was just wanting to make me feel better. That is class.

Suddenly Dad started to fish around under his false teeth with his tongue. He poked the top set out of his mouth while he tried to remove a bit of food that had lodged there. The skin stretched over his cheeks so that his face looked like a hundred-year-old skull dug up from the desert.

It was the longest night of my life. I was torn between wanting to be close to Charlie and feeling sick that she'd never come near me after this. Finally she got up to go.

Outside, Charlie slowly put on her skis. 'I'll walk you home,' I said.

'There's no need, Robin. It's not very far.' She turned to Dad. 'Thank you for having me round,' she said with that beautiful smile of hers.

I noted that she didn't say, 'Thank you for a lovely evening' or 'Thank you for the delicious meal'.

It's Saturday, the day before I'm to go to Charlie's for dinner. Dad's outside trying to free the snowmobile that I forgot to take back to the Integrity Chairlift Company after he'd fixed it for them. He's not too happy because that's my job. The snowmobile is sheeted with ice and Dad's pouring hot water over the tracks to try and free it. Finally the ice loosens its grip and he pushes it back inside the workshop next to his own machine, a 2006 three-seater Ski-Doo GTX which he maintains in perfect condition. He loves getting out there on the Ski-Doo with the Mountain Rescue guys who need him in case some of their equipment breaks down mid-rescue.

He gestures towards the back door. 'Hop into the woodpile, Robin,' he orders. 'See if you can finish the lot.' He's wearing his balaclava to keep the cold off his ears and bald patch and I can only see his eyes and mouth. He looks like he's off to hold up a bank. Behind the workshop is a pile of snow-gum logs. Two tonnes of them.

'Can I do it tomorrow, Dad? I've got a lot of homework this weekend.'

'Homework! Writing more of your nonsense more like it. You don't want *me* to chop it, do you? Not with this bad back.'

There's no point arguing so I head for the woodpile. I don't get paid for chopping wood, which is part of my 'chores'. I get ten dollars an hour for helping in the workshop on holidays and weekends.

'The minimum wage is fifteen dollars an hour,' I said to him once.

'It's related to intelligence,' was his reply.

I face the pile of snow-covered logs stacked between the workshop and our lodge. Snow gum is the worst sort of wood to chop. I have to whack the big logs three or four times with the axe before they'll split. Even with gloves on, my hands freeze up and the wood is so hard that the axe bounces off sending great judders of pain up my arms. But the real reason I hate doing it is because of what happens inside my head – it's the champagne corks exploding. I can't chop wood without setting them off. I hate them, I hate them, I hate them. Unpredictable images that pop into my mind. I can feel them stirring in my brain. It's the axe that causes them.

I haven't got very far before I have to throw the axe down onto the snow and begin to cart the wood to the back porch to take my mind off things.

After a hard day working for the old man I go up to my room and shut the door. Although our house is shabby and untidy it does have a sort of safe, warm, rustic feel because of the wooden floors and walls and high cathedral ceilings. And my room's the cosiest of all.

I have a computer on a table in the corner and bookshelves on three walls. The shelves are all bulging because every time I go down the mountain to Bright Dale I spend my money on secondhand books and I've got heaps of them – mostly fiction. My favourites at the moment are *Huckleberry Finn* and *The Road*, which is a story about a boy and his father who tries to save him from predators when there's no food left in the world.

My room is where I write stories on long winter nights. It's a way of getting away from the old man. When I'm lost in writing a story I forget all about him. I just let my imagination go. Ideas suddenly jump into my head and I type them up. I haven't a clue where they come from – they're just stories.

In one corner there's an old dressing-table with two drawers below and a mirror above. I pull the bottom drawer right out revealing a space underneath which is my secret hiding place for things I don't want Dad to know about. There's a photo of Charlie that I cut out of the school magazine. If she knew I had it she'd probably take it from me and say, 'Robin, we're just friends', and I'd die of embarrassment and shame and even worse I would know for sure there could never be anything between us. I can't work her out – she seems to enjoy talking with me, but then she might just be being polite. I touch the place where she brushed me with her lips. It was the kiss of a feather floating on the breeze. I smile at the thought of it. I would give everything I have for one proper kiss from her. I start to imagine what it would be like but the thought is rudely removed by another one: if I don't come up with five hundred dollars, I'm history as far as she's concerned.

In the hiding place there's also a hairbrush and a ring that once belonged to my mother. The ring is white gold with a clasp shaped like a hand, holding a tiny diamond. The hairbrush is an antique, made of blue glass with black bristles which still have two or three strands of Mum's long red hair entwined in them. I found the ring and the brush a couple of years ago when I was emptying the rubbish and I'm pretty sure the old man had thrown them out in a temper. He won't talk about

Mum or where she is and he freaks out if I mention her name. There are no photos of her but I do have a picture of what she looked like in my mind. This can't be a real memory because I was only a baby when she left but I somehow know that my imaginings are true. I take the ring out of its hiding spot and place it on my pillow. The ring and the hairbrush are my most treasured possessions. I'll never part with either of them, especially the ring because it reminds me of a mother's eternal love which can never be tarnished. I wish I knew where she was. I can't remember ever having been held close by a woman but I can imagine what it might be like. Mum's touch would be softer than a marshmallow.

*Kerbang*. The door flies open and Dad follows it in like a hurricane. He never knocks on my door even though I've asked him to a million times.

'Have you taken my . . .' His voice trails off and his eyes fix on the ring. He strides across the room, snatches it up and rushes to the window.

'No,' I yell.

He shoves up the window letting a wall of cold air

rush in and throws the ring out into the night. I don't even see it go. The ring vanishes like a coin swallowed by the ocean.

'I don't want her memory in this house,' he says angrily. 'You know that.'

'I don't *have* any memories of her,' I say.

I rush down the stairs, his hoarse laugh echoing behind me. I pull on my snow gear, snatch up a torch from the kitchen and plunge into the whiteness of the black night. The snow is crusty and brittle like the icing on an old cake. I stand and think about the best way to search, knowing that if I stomp around I might crush the ring into the bed of mud under the snow and then I'll never find it. A flash of brilliance hits me. I run to the workshop, take Dad's metal detector from its place on the wall and start searching the ground, sweeping the snow systematically in rows.

*Beep*. My heart leaps as I drop to my knees and dig at the spot with my glove. A brass button. Bugger. An hour passes and then another. By this time I've collected a fifty-cent piece, the tip of a ski pole, four nails and one baked-beans can. I'm shivering badly but nothing will stop me searching until I find my mother's ring. The house lights all die as Dad goes to bed. He thinks I'll never find the ring but he hasn't taken into account the metal detector, which we both know I'm not allowed to touch. I traverse the yard for hours, swishing the detector from side to side without a break. In all I've accumulated about twenty useless metal items. Some of them have been buried in the frozen earth for years and I've had to chip them out with a screwdriver and hammer. In the end I fall helplessly onto the ground shaking with cold and anger. I can't live without her ring. I can't live without her hairbrush. They're all I have until I find her. And something tells me that one day they'll lead me to her – then they won't matter anymore.

I'll have to come back in the morning when there's daylight. Sagging with frustration and sorrow I drag myself up to my room and take off my wet clothes. As I do so, I glimpse a twinkle of light on my pillow. It's the ring! My head swirls as I try to make sense of it, and then it dawns on me: Dad only pretended to throw the ring out of the window.

Corks pop inside my head as if fired from a shotgun.

Smoke from the ski-lodge chimneys curls into the night air and turns the moon blood red. The ranger's home where Charlie lives is a huge wooden cabin spreading out through the trees. Snow lies thickly on the roof and icicles hang from the eaves. The cabin is surrounded by a scattering of huts and cages and animal enclosures, all clothed in white. As I glide between them on my skis I see two large eyes blink from inside a black aviary. A powerful owl.

Charlie's father keeps injured wildlife in these enclosures and nurses them back to health. They all have names: Maggie, a koala that was burnt in a bushfire; Josephine, a wallaby that was found still alive in its dead mother's pouch; and Squawk, a parrot with a broken wing. There's also a poor old wombat called Alf, who was hit by a car – Charlie invited me round to see him once. As I near the homestead I see that Alf's cage is empty.

Charlie meets me at the front door. She looks even more lovely in her soft jumper and jeans but her eyes are moist.

'Charlie, what's up?' I say. 'What's happened?'

She forces a smile. 'Nothing. It's fine. I'm fine. Come on in.'

'Are you all right?' I ask as I bend down to take off my skis.

She changes the subject. 'You look good in that leather jacket,' she says. 'But aren't you cold?'

I *am* a bit cold and I should have worn full snow gear but I wanted to look my best. I have a balaclava tucked in my pocket in case the weather turns bad on the way home.

'Thanks,' I say. 'I'm okay.'

I hand over my jacket and lean my skis against the wall. We go inside into the warm and I'm introduced to

Charlie's parents: Russell, who has a close-cut beard, wild hair and a friendly smile; and Louise, who is the calm and unruffable type. She wears no make-up and a little bit of grey is starting to show in her dark hair. Charlie's grandpa, Fred, has a face that's wrinkled like a dried-out chamois leather, with two eyes that could easily belong to a cheeky ten-year-old peering out from the creases.

It feels weird when I sit down with a proper family at a table set out with napkins and matching cutlery. Weird but nice. The fire's burning happily. Outside snowflakes flit briefly past the window and vanish into the darkness like dancers leaving a stage. The scene reminds me of something out of an English Christmas card except there are no fir trees and it's a long time until Christmas in Australia. Russell is dishing up roasted vegetables and Louise pours drinks.

'Moose will be here soon,' says Grandpa.

'*That'll* be lovely,' says Louise with a tinge of irony.

Charlie laughs. 'No more stories, Grandpa. We've heard them all ten times before.'

'I hear you've been very generous in regard to the Somalis,' says Louise. 'Is your dad okay with that?'

'I work for my money,' I say, 'so what I do with it is up to me.' Louise doesn't look convinced but she lets it go.

'Everyone's so excited,' says Charlie. 'I've already phoned Melbourne and told the support group the news. The kids have never seen snow before.' She throws me a warm smile.

I groan inwardly – I'll never get five hundred dollars – it might as well be a billion. I open my mouth to mumble something but at this very moment Moose comes in. His face is nearly as wrinkled as Grandpa's and he's bald and only seems to have about three teeth. He grabs my hand.

'Moose,' he says.

'Robin,' I say.

'You're late,' says Grandpa.

'Bulldust,' says Moose. 'You're early.'

'I live here, mate.'

They eye each other off with wicked smiles. Charlie laughs.

'Go for it, everyone,' says Russell. I pick up my knife and fork uncertainly. I'm a bit nervous because I want to create a good impression and I'm still not quite sure how to behave sitting around a table like this and I don't want to look like an idiot in front of Charlie. But everyone else is hopping straight into it, so I do the same. It's a fantastic feast with steak and sausages and roasted pumpkin and carrots.

I feel as if I should contribute to the conversation. 'Where's Alf?' I say. 'Did you let him go?'

The mood in the room plunges. It's as if I've opened a fridge door and cold air has spilled across the table. No one speaks, then finally:

'Dad killed him,' says Charlie.

I gasp.

'Charlie!' exclaims Louise.

'That's not fair,' says Russell. 'I *had* to put him down, Robin.'

'What happened?' I ask. I'm shocked.

'He was suffering terribly. I had to end his misery.'

'How?' I say foolishly. Of course I know how.

'A simple injection. He slowly fell asleep. Didn't feel a thing.'

'You could've tried,' says Charlie, barely containing her distress. 'I know you've had to do it many times, Dad, but Alf was part of the family. You could have waited a bit longer.'

'But at what cost, Charlie? Poor Alf was in agony. Sometimes you don't have a choice in these things.'

'Alf is the one who didn't have a choice,' says Charlie. Her lips are quivering.

'If it was me,' says Grandpa, '*I* would choose the needle.'

'That's right,' says Moose seriously. 'In the war there was this bloke who had his legs . . .'

He stops. Louise is glaring at him. Her head inclines towards me as if to indicate that I'm too sensitive to hear a graphic description of someone getting their legs blown off. If only she knew what graphic images I've already had to cope with.

'When *my* time comes,' says Grandpa, 'I give you permission to put me down. I've signed a paper.'

'Did Alf sign a paper?' says Charlie. 'No one asked what he thought.'

'Animals don't think,' says Russell. 'You know that.'

'How do you know?'

'They don't have choices. You have control over your mind and your actions. But if an animal is hungry, it eats when it sees food. It has no choice. It doesn't think about it.'

'Do we have control over our thoughts?' I ask. 'Things just pop into your head from nowhere, don't they?'

'That's my point,' says Russell. 'As humans we can choose.'

'If it's what we *do* that counts,' says Charlie, 'then Dad's responsible for killing Alf.'

'I took a decision for the sake of a poor dumb creature,' says Russell. 'You would do it yourself.'

'No I wouldn't,' says Charlie.

Charlie and Russell both stare down at their plates. The only sound is of cutlery on crockery, and a bit of chomping from Moose. Eventually Louise breaks the silence.

'What do you think, Robin?'

'Dad says I think too much,' I say, neatly sidestepping her question.

'I don't think enough sometimes,' says Charlie. 'I'm sorry, Dad. I know you loved Alf too, and it was the only thing to do and you tried your best to save him. I know it sometimes has to be done but I can never get used to it.'

'I didn't just do it on impulse,' says Russell. 'I thought about it long and hard. But I'm sorry too. I should have given you more warning.'

They smile at each other and Russell reaches across the table and Charlie does the same and they clasp hands with tears in their eyes.

There's a sort of embarrassed but pleased silence around the table. Grandpa speaks again.

'In the war . . .'

'No!' shrieks Louise. 'Not this again, Dad.'

'In the war,' he says, ignoring her and winking at me, 'you couldn't get steak like this. I remember a time when all I had to eat was five small raisins.'

Moose grabs the lifebelt that Grandpa has thrown us. 'But not as small as his nuts,' he yelps.

Everyone laughs and from then on the evening flies by. I hardly seem to have settled in when it's time to go home. I thank Russell and Louise for the delicious meal, say goodbye to Grandpa and Moose and step outside into the cold night with Charlie. She's so beautiful that I can hardly breathe as I put on my skis.

The moon has sprinkled the snow with a million diamonds. The air is clear and crisp and I can feel the cold snapping at my ears. I take my balaclava out of my jacket pocket and pull it over my face.

'Well, that was a great night,' I say quickly because even though I don't want to leave Charlie, I have to get away before she has a chance to ask me about the money. 'Thanks so much . . .' I start to say.

Charlie holds one finger up to her lips. She closes her eyes and turns her face up to mine. She wants me to kiss her! I rip off my balaclava and as I do I see that it's Dad's. I must have grabbed his by mistake. There's a rim of his dried white spit on the edge of the mouth hole.

Charlie's standing there with her face tilted up and her eyes closed, gently smiling and waiting. But a picture is forming in the depths. It's going to erupt like a cork out of a bottle. It's going to ruin the moment. Hell.

I have to run. It's the only way to stop it. The sickening image builds up in my head like a shaken bottle of champagne.

I dig my stocks into the snow and push off, my skis biting into the powder as I swoosh down the slope leaving Charlie there kissing the bloody moon.

I lost my chance.

And the cork popped anyway.

# The Habit

There were four basic rules in the monastery.

1 *No monk may enter The Door of His Desire*

2 *No monk may drink alcohol*

3 *No monk may make love to a woman*

4 *No monk may pray for himself*

Brother Gordon had trouble with Rule Number Two. He had been a monk for twenty-five years but he still wanted a bottle of champagne more than any other pleasure. He dreamed of champagne. He thought of champagne night and day. He was tortured by images of bottles of champagne. He longed for a drink.

Brother Theo had trouble with Rule Number Three. He had been a monk for ten years but he still longed for a woman more than any other pleasure.

Every evening Brother Theo lay on his hard wooden bed and dreamed of naked women. He thought of bare breasts night and day. When he conjured up a naked woman in his mind all other thoughts disappeared. If only he could have the real thing all his troubles would be over.

Every evening Brother Gordon lay on his hard wooden bed and dreamed of champagne. He fought with the images of champagne that filled his mind but he couldn't get rid of them. He was in agony. The more he thought about not thinking about champagne the more the pictures formed in his head. One night, he could stand it no longer: he knelt by his bed and broke Rule Number Four.

'Oh, God,' he cried out. 'Please deliver me from this torture. Give me a drink of grog.'

Brother Gordon rose from his knees and saw a large black key attached to his habit belt by a chain. He had never seen it before but he knew at once which door the key opened.

That night he lit a candle and quietly snuck along the corridor to The Door of His Desire. Without taking the key from his belt he inserted it into the lock. The door swung open before him. He saw a flight of stone steps leading down to an enormous cellar. Brother Gordon quietly closed the door behind him and crept down the steps. To his delight he found that the cellar walls were lined with at least one thousand bottles of the finest champagne.

Overhead was a large sign which said:

*KNEEL*

*AND*

*RECITE THE POEM*

*'THE RIME OF THE ANCIENT MARINER'*

*BEFORE DRINKING A BOTTLE*

The poem was written out in full beneath the sign. It appeared to have around a hundred and fifty verses, most with four lines per verse.

Brother Gordon salivated. He had not had a drink for a quarter of a century. The bottles called to him like sirens. He could remember some of the poem from his days at school. It was something about a sailor who was adrift on a ship that had run out of drinking water.

Like the mariner of old, Brother Gordon couldn't wait for a

drink. He reached for the nearest bottle but just as his hand was about to close on the neck, the cork shot out and sprayed the champagne all over him. The contents were totally wasted.

He reached for the next bottle in the rack but the same thing happened and the cork shot out like a cannon ball. Poor Brother Gordon was soaked once more.

This time he decided to obey the sign. He knelt and began to recite the poem. He read quickly but by the time he reached the end of Part I, the demon drink began to call him loudly indeed. He tried to ignore it and read on:

*God save thee, ancient Mariner,*
*From the fiends that plague thee thus! –*
*Why look'st thou so? – 'With my crossbow*
*I shot the Albatross.'*

Brother Gordon couldn't wait any longer. He ran to the wine rack to grab a bottle but it exploded in his face.

'Damn,' he said. He dropped back to his knees and continued reading:

*And I had done a hellish thing,*
*And it would work 'em woe:*
*For all averred, I had killed the bird*
*That made the breeze to blow.*
*Ah wretch! said they, the bird to slay,*
*That made the breeze to blow!*

Brother Gordon's throat grew dry but he read on:

*Water, water, everywhere,*
*And all the boards did shrink;*
*Water, water, everywhere,*
*Nor any drop to drink.*

Oh, the word 'drink' nearly drove Brother Gordon crazy but he ploughed on until he had finished all one hundred and forty-four verses of the poem. It had taken him half an hour.

He lunged for a bottle, grabbed it and popped the cork. He drank the contents. It made his head spin. Brother Gordon would have liked another bottle but he was exhausted. He couldn't read even one more verse. He walked up the steps, locked the cellar door behind him and quietly made his way, unseen, back to his tiny cell.

The next night Brother Gordon was again tortured by thoughts of champagne. He crept silently along the corridor and let himself into the cellar of a thousand bottles. He knelt and recited 'The Rime of the Ancient Mariner' without stopping. Then, with trembling fingers, he reached for a bottle of champagne. Before he could touch it, the cork shot out and sprayed him with the contents. The alcohol was wasted. He tried again and the same thing happened. There was only one thing to do. Hurriedly Brother Gordon began to recite the terrible poem for a second time that night:

*Ah! well-a-day! what evil looks*
*Had I from old and young!*
*Instead of the cross, the Albatross*
*About my neck was hung.*

The words tumbled out until he was finished. Immediately Brother Gordon reached for another bottle and grasped it firmly. He removed the cork and drank the contents. His head grew light from the bubbles. Once again he crept back to his cell. He knew in his heart that to get the third bottle he would have to recite the poem three times. It was the way this demon worked.

On the third night Brother Gordon recited the poem three times and was rewarded with a beautiful bottle of champagne.

On the fourth night Brother Gordon recited the poem four times and was rewarded with another fine bottle. On the fifth night Brother Gordon recited 'The Rime of the Ancient Mariner' five times. And on the sixth he recited it six times. Each time he was rewarded with an unexploded bottle. The verses spun crazily in his head:

*The very deep did rot: O Christ!*
*That ever this should be!*
*Yea, slimy things did crawl with legs*
*Upon the slimy sea!*

Each reading of the whole poem took around half an hour. By the tenth night Brother Gordon was growing tired. It hardly seemed worth reciting 'The Rime of the Ancient Mariner' ten times just for one bottle of champagne. But by this time the demon drink had him by the balls and he couldn't stop himself. He hesitantly made a few attempts at opening a bottle without reciting the poem the correct number of times but it always exploded in his face.

As the days passed Brother Gordon grew weaker and weaker. His knees were red from kneeling before the bottles. He looked along the rows of champagne and knew that this could not continue. More and more of each night was being gobbled up by the recitations. But he was hooked. He wanted to stop the repetitive poetry readings but his desire for drink was too strong.

Brother Gordon was good at maths and figured out that on the sixteenth night he would be spending eight hours reciting before the bottles. He would get no sleep at all. Something had to be done. He couldn't stay up every night reading the poem. The poor monk was desperate. If there was no champagne he would not be able to drink it.

On the sixteenth night Brother Gordon reached out for a bottle of champagne without reciting. It sprayed all over him wasting the contents. He touched the next bottle and the same thing happened. Quickly he moved along the racks touching each bottle in turn. Explosions filled the air like shots from a repeating rifle as he hurried along the rows. The floor ran with champagne. His habit was drenched. But in the end every bottle was exhausted. There was not another drop to be had.

He crept up the stairs and paused to look back. To his amazement he saw that the racks of champagne had gone. In their place were a thousand beds and on each bed was a naked woman. Brother Gordon shook his head and made a vow never to return. A single verse echoed in his head as he left:

*He went like one that hath been stunned,*
*And is of sense forlorn:*
*A sadder and a wiser man*
*He rose the morrow morn.*

The monk hurriedly stepped out of The Door of His Desire for the last time. He reached for the key but found that it was no longer hanging from his belt. The door had locked itself. The first rays of sunrise glowed from a high window in the corridor. An image of a full bottle of champagne floated into Brother Gordon's head.

'Damn it,' he said.

He decided to leave the monastery forever. Just to be on

the safe side. Running away from the problem seemed to be the only way of avoiding it.

At that moment he saw a figure lurking nearby. It was Brother Theo who had been watching from the shadows.

'Have you been through The Door of Your Desire, Brother Gordon?' he asked.

Brother Gordon nodded guiltily.

Brother Theo grinned and held up a black key. 'I have prayed for my heart's desire and have the key,' he said eagerly. 'What will I get beyond the door, Brother?'

An image of the thousand naked women flitted across Brother Gordon's mind. 'More than you expect, Brother Theo,' he said. 'More than you expect.'

# THE NEST

## 2

It's a week since I left Charlie kissing the moon. Dad and I drive down the mountain in his old Land Rover to Bright Dale. We need groceries and supplies for the workshop. We travel without speaking because Dad needs to concentrate when he's driving on icy roads. This suits me fine because I've got so many problems to think about. Ever since I ran away from Charlie I've been weighed down by guilt. I insulted her. If I turn what happened around and imagine that I'd had the guts to try and kiss *her* and *she'd* turned away, I'd have been so humiliated that I'd never have been able to look at her again. And, to make it even worse, I still haven't got the money I promised her.

I put my hand inside my T-shirt and wrap my fingers around Mum's ring. Because the old man knows I have it, I keep it on a chain around my neck. Feeling it now gets me thinking. I create a little picture in my mind where I'm giving it to Charlie as an engagement ring. It's a few years down the track and I've just published a book that has instantly become a bestseller. Charlie has finished university and we're both free to do whatever we like. She's thrilled when she sees the ring and throws her arms around my neck with joy.

I'd have to take the ring to the jeweller's and have it professionally cleaned first though.

My daydream is rudely interrupted when Dad hits the brakes at a set of traffic lights. We're there. He pulls into the car park behind the main street and then takes off to buy some tools and have a drink in the pub.

'Don't waste your money on books and crap that just fills your head with nonsense,' he says.

'What money?' I say. He doesn't take the hint.

Bright Dale has more shops every time we visit. The highway to Sydney cuts straight through the middle of the town but there's talk of creating a bypass which the locals don't want. The shops, including those that hire out ski gear, snow chains and warm clothing line the road together with cafés and places flogging souvenirs to the throngs of tourists. A supermarket and a cluster of office buildings are behind the main street to the north. Just outside town to the east is the school and to the west is the industrial area. There are three pubs – Dad's favourite watering hole is The Vic.

Expensive cars with skis on the roof hardly slow as they roar through the town. The caffelatte crowd don't stop in Bright Dale; they own all their own gear and have everything they need for a week on the slopes. The day visitors with kids mostly hire their equipment down here because it's cheaper than on the mountain.

I pass a family standing around an old station wagon warming themselves with thick mugs of coffee poured from a thermos. My feet take me slowly to the place that I've been thinking about for most of the morning. I push open the door of the jeweller's shop and wait while a guy and his girlfriend are being served. They're buying a wedding ring and take ages looking at just about everything in the shop. After what seems like forever they leave without making a purchase. My hand trembles as I put my mother's engagement ring on the counter in front of the owner and I hear myself utter the saddest words of my life: 'How much?'

The jeweller, who is a middle-aged guy, doesn't seem too happy that he just missed a sale. He picks up my ring and examines it through a magnifying glass. Then he looks at me over the top of his glasses. 'It's worth around four hundred. Maybe a little more. Whose is it anyway?'

'My mother's.' I can hardly believe I just said that.

'I can't buy it without her permission,' he says, handing it back to me.

'She's . . . gone,' I say, blinking quickly as tears threaten to fill my eyes.

'Your father then. I'm sorry, son, but it could be

stolen. Do you want to sell it or not? You'll have to bring your father in. I can't buy it without ID showing the name and address of the adult who's selling it.'

'Please, it's really important. It's mine, I swear it. My mother left it to me when my parents split up.'

He shakes his head. 'Can't do it, son. Sorry.'

I emerge into the crisp air and the bright sunshine where the mood of the happy weekend crowd just increases my inner misery. At least I've still got the ring. I vowed I'd never part with it, and I won't.

But then this tiny glow of imaginary warmth is extinguished. I'll never make it up to Charlie if I can't sell it – she won't forgive me for a second betrayal. I start to talk to myself, putting the case for each side:

— Try to sell the ring. Get Dad to sign the papers.

— Forget about Charlie. She's only a girl. The ring might lead me to my mother.

— But what about the Somali kids? They're already looking forward to their holiday. And Charlie will look like an idiot when she can't produce the money.

— Mum wouldn't want me to sell her ring.

—Yes, she would. She would understand. She's my mother.

I feel like a trapped rat – whichever way I turn I'll hurt someone. It's a lose-lose situation.

I take a fifty-cent coin out of my pocket and run my fingers around its edges. I could toss up and let fate decide – heads I keep the ring and tails I approach Dad to sign the papers. He'd be glad to get rid of the ring once and for all. I realise with a start that I'm standing outside Jackson's second-hand bookshop, looking in the window without knowing it. I'm staring at an old book. The author's name is in big print at the top: Noel Coward.

Coward! That's me. The name is telling me something. I have to make the decision about the ring myself. Tossing up is a coward's way out. I can't just spin a coin and then blame the result on fate. My eye travels to the title of the book: *Look After Lulu*. Another alliterative title springs into my mind: *Choose Charlie.* Suddenly I know what I have to do. Charlie and the kids from Somalia are more important than an object, even if it's a precious ring, and no matter how much I love her, Mum's gone and I have to accept it.

I walk to the pub where Dad's sitting in a corner drinking a light beer. The Vic is the only pub in town that doesn't have ready-cooked food and heaps of tables for the hungry hordes of skiers when they head home from the snowfields. It's tucked into a back street and inside is quite small with just one long bar and carpet that stinks of stale beer. A few farmers and truckies sit on stools at the counter. At the end of the room is a large screen flickering with the violent images of a boxing match. The blows make me wince and I try not to look. I place the ring on the table. The old man stares at it. One of his eyebrows starts to twitch.

'What?' he growls. Behind his thick glasses his eyes are smouldering.

'The jeweller's offered me four hundred dollars for it – maybe a little more. I need your permission.'

'You're selling it? The thing you searched for all night in the snow? That you vowed never to part with? I don't believe it. What do you want the money for? Have you got that girl pregnant? Or is it drugs? Good grief, as if I haven't got enough troubles already.'

'Dad, it's nothing like that. I just want to sell it, that's all. I know how much it upsets you.'

His eyebrow stops twitching. He seems pleased at this news. 'Let's go.'

'You'll need ID,' I tell him.

He drains his glass and we march over to the jeweller's. 'This is mine,' he says curtly, putting the ring on the counter and slapping his driver's licence down. 'I want five hundred for it. That's less than half what I paid for it in the first place. Take it or leave it.'

The two men look at each other and the jeweller decides that my father won't negotiate. He reaches under the counter, takes out a form and places it on the bench.

'Fill this in while I get your money.'

I'm relieved that I'll soon have the money for Charlie, but I feel as if I've sold my mother's soul. I've eased one pain by creating another. The weight in my heart has grown even heavier.

Dad walks out with me, counting the money as he goes. He peels off a one hundred dollar note and hands it to me.

'Here you go,' he says. 'Like I said, don't fritter it away on nothing.'

'I need it all,' I say, feeling the old resentment rising.

'What you want and what you get are two different things.'

'It's my ring, not yours. You never wanted it, you threw it out.'

'I bought it,' he says. 'And I want my money back. Think yourself lucky you've got a hundred.'

Defiantly I start to walk back into the shop.

'Where are you going?' he demands.

'I'm going to tell the jeweller it's stolen. He'll call the police.'

I've never stood up to him like this before. He's quivering with anger but I can tell there's more to it than that.

An old lady with a pram has stopped and is listening to the exchange as if it's a bit of street theatre.

'Have it your own way,' he snaps. 'Selfish as always, just like your mother.'

He suddenly drops the rest of the money onto the ground without a word and storms off towards the supermarket to buy the groceries. Why did he change his mind? What is he scared of?

The journey home is hideous. The feelings of resentment between me and Dad kill any form of communication for the first hour or so. Not that I care. I've got plenty to think about anyway. I did the right thing by selling the ring. I never break a promise, and it's good to help the Somalis. But it hurts. It hurts bad. Just as we reach the snowline the old man suddenly pulls the car to the side of the road and switches off the motor.

'You've got her hairbrush too, haven't you?' he growls.

'No,' I say instinctively. There's no way I'm giving him the hairbrush.

'Ha!' he exclaims.

'What?'

'You glanced up. A liar always glances up before they speak.'

'Try me again.'

He thinks about this for a few seconds and his face hardens.

'Okay, repeat after me: "I do not have my mother's hairbrush".'

I fix my eyes on the steering wheel. 'I do not have my mother's hairbrush.'

He nods his head and goes on.

'If this is not true . . .'

'If this is not true . . .'

'May I die a horrible death.'

My mouth is dry. 'May I . . .'

I can't say it. I just can't form the words. And I can't believe that he is doing this. It's like some childish schoolyard ritual but there's a sinister reality behind his words.

'So you've got the brush,' he says.

I nod and he gives a satisfied smirk as he turns the ignition key and starts the car. I reach over and twist the key, killing the engine.

'Now it's my turn.'

He regards me like a poker player calling someone's bluff.

'Fair enough.'

'Do you know where my mother is?'

He freezes. Then *he* fixes his eyes on the steering wheel.

'No.'

'If this is not true . . .'

'If this is not true,' he repeats slowly.

'May I die a horrible death.'

He doesn't hesitate but continues in the same measured tone.

'May I die a horrible death.'

I am left speechless. I should have asked him why he gave me the rest of the money when I mentioned the police. But there's no second chance in this game. Something awful has happened. But I don't know what it is.

That night in bed I toss and turn and don't really get to sleep until just before dawn. I have a crazy dream that a group of Somali children are falling out of a high window one after the other. I rush from one to the next trying unsuccessfully to catch them before they hit the ground. Finally only Charlie is left. She is desperately hanging onto the windowsill by one hand. She loses her grip and begins to fall. I rush forward to catch her but before I can, this senseless nightmare ends and I wake up in a terrified sweat.

I know that I won't rest until I've given Charlie the money. As soon as the old man goes out I pick up the phone and dial. Russell answers.

'She's not here at the moment, Robin,' he says. 'She's been a bit down lately – must be still grieving over poor old Alf.'

'I need to talk to her,' I say, trying not to sound too desperate.

'You might have to wait a bit. She's gone walking to cheer herself up. I'll get her to call you back.'

'No, don't, Russell. I might go and look for her. Do you know where she was headed?'

'The forest, I expect, Robin. That's where she usually goes. Good luck.'

I say goodbye and hang up. If mobiles worked up here in the mountains I could ring her. I go and get my parka with the five hundred dollars safe inside the zip pocket but as usual the old man has other ideas.

'Where do you think you're going?' he says as he observes me from the workshop door. 'You know I'm flat out at the moment. Get in here, now.' He starts tinkering around with a snowmobile that's been brought in with a broken exhaust pipe.

'Yeah, I will, Dad. I've just got to see Charlie first,' I say. 'It's important.'

'Work's more important than girls,' he says. 'Go find the tape measure and don't be sullen about it. Show me a bit of respect for once. There's no point arguing. Chatting up Charlie will have to wait.'

I look at the littered workshop bench. Somewhere in the mess is the tape measure and he can't get on with cutting a new exhaust pipe without it. I start rummaging around amongst the junk.

'Well, what are you doing? Haven't you found it yet?'

'I'm looking, I'm looking. It's not here.'

'You're obviously not looking properly,' he yells. 'Concentrate. Stop dreaming about that girl.'

By now I've tidied the whole bench up. I've put the metal shavings from the lathe in the bin, the spanners are all back in their box and I have sorted out the nuts and bolts and put them into their jars, but still no tape measure.

'Hurry up,' he says. 'I told Integrity they could have their machine back this afternoon.'

He's wearing his old boilersuit as usual. It has pockets everywhere and they all bulge with the tools he's stuffed into them.

Dare I ask him THE question? Yes I will: I've had enough. 'Could it be in your pocket?'

'Don't be an imbecile,' he snarls. 'I haven't used it today.'

'Maybe it's still there from the last time. Just have a look.'

He glares at me.

'Please, Dad. I've looked everywhere.'

He gives an annoyed sigh, pats one pocket and pulls out the lost tape measure. He measures the exhaust pipe and throws the tape back to me.

'Put it back in its proper place,' he says.

I work till lunchtime, taking the motor out of a snowmobile which blew up after someone used it to drag a fallen gum tree. Four hours is the deal I have with the old man, so at last I can go.

'I'm off to see Charlie now,' I say.

'Light the pot-belly stove first,' he says. 'It's freezing.'

I fetch some logs and split kindling and then fill the pot belly which stands against the workshop wall. I put a match to it and it bursts into crackling flames. Dad picks up the poker and shoves it into the fire, sending sparks flying. His body completely blocks the heat. As he jabs at the wood an image of the poker in my own hand flashes into my head.

'You're making it worse,' I say. 'It's going out.'

'Chop a few more logs for me, Robin.'

'I can't, Dad. I've got to go and find Charlie.'

'Oh, all right then,' he says. 'Do it tomorrow. I'll just stay here and work in the freezing cold.'

He wags the poker at me and takes a breath. I know what's coming.

'When I was your age my mother was dead and I was working in a factory helping to support my invalid father. You don't know the meaning of work. You're bone idle, Robin.'

Oh, god. I can't stand this. I just lose it. I can't help myself and I give him a bit of his own medicine back.

'If I knew where *my* mother was I'd go and live with her like a shot and I'd work my butt off to support her. She wouldn't carry on like you do. She probably left because you're a bully.'

This hits him where it hurts. 'She – left – be – cause – of – *you*,' he spits out, beating down with the poker to emphasise every syllable.

He has named my greatest fear. Why didn't she take me with her? Wasn't I good enough?

Seeing that poker waving around is agony. I use every bit of mental energy I can to stop a violent image from forming inside my head, and I try to head it off by running out of the workshop. But I don't escape. Like a bite from a snake, I'm hit with an image of myself whacking the poker into my father's skull.

Horrible, horrible, horrible.

Charlie's probably heading for home by now. I frantically put on my full snow outfit and grab my emergency pack in case the weather turns lethal. I ski uphill out of the village and head for the forest where the wilderness will calm my racing mind.

Charlie often skis the forest trails so if she hasn't gone home I might be able to find her and give her the money. And with a bit of luck she might forgive me for leaving her standing there kissing the moon. I make good progress and soon leave the tourists, the shouting and the yobbos far behind. At this time in the afternoon the forest is as quiet as a tomb. I relive a thousand times the feel of her lips on my cheek and the warm glow that flowed through my body. I imagine what a proper kiss would have been like.

I've been going for about half an hour when I see

something move just off the track. A movement like the fluttering of an eyelid, something small. It's a little blue wren and it's badly hurt. A hawk or something must have injured it. One wing looks broken. I think it might be dying. I take off my gloves and gently pick up the injured bird. I can feel its heart beating weakly. Its head is bent to one side, eyes staring rigidly ahead, resigned to its fate. There's nothing I can do for this tiny creature except . . .

Oh, help, not that. I can't do it. I can't do the unspeakable. But I can't abandon the poor thing either. I try to talk myself out of what must be done. Animals die every day, thousands of them – millions. Hawks eat smaller birds. Small birds eat live worms. It's the way of nature. But I'm not a dumb animal. I can't just leave the wren to a slow death and walk off with a clear conscience. I have to kill it. I can't bring myself to do it, though. I just can't. But I must.

Near by is a puddle. Its frozen skin has started to melt. I slide quickly to the icy water and lower the wren below the surface. Cold needles sting my fingers but through the pain I feel the heart of the little bird pump twice and then stop. I hold the fragile body in the freezing water until I can't stand it any longer, then I gently place the wet and lifeless remains of the bird inside a nearby hollow log, put my gloves back on and continue on my numb journey, wishing that Charlie had been with me to share the decision.

After a couple more hours skiing I still haven't found her and I think she must have gone home. I reach the summit and head down towards the boarded-up shaft known as Jacob's Mine. The slope is bare of all vegetation until the trail descends into the forest again and passes Deep Lake and the turn-off to Logan's Refuge – an emergency storm shelter.

When I reach the refuge I brush the snow off a boulder and sit down to eat the chocolates and bananas I've brought with me. I'll need the energy to get back home. It's incredibly peaceful here looking through the snow gums to the valleys below and the endless ridges of mountains. The stillness calms my mind but I can't stay because the afternoon is beginning to fade. I ski back up to the summit and am soon on the narrow track through the forest.

The bent trees submit to the weight of soft snow. What secrets do these white coats cover? My mind begins to wander and by now I'm totally absorbed in these thoughts as I ski back down the trail. That's why I take a few seconds to recognise the figure in the red parka. Oh my god, it's her. There she is, sitting on a log that's vaguely familiar. She's as calm as someone waiting for a bus. My heart starts to pound and I can hardly breathe. It's as if my skis are frozen to the ground. I feel like, I don't know . . . like if I move I'll disturb the molecules that are holding her together.

'Hello,' she says. She isn't smiling. 'Fancy meeting *you* here.'

I don't know what to say. The words I find so easily when I write a story dry up the moment a girl comes near me.

She looks at me for a while as if to say 'So?'.

'What are you doing here?' I croak.

'I've been losing myself in the forest.' She thinks

about this and then corrects herself. 'Finding myself, maybe. What are you doing?'

I glance up at the sky. 'Just cruising.' I give a nervous laugh.

'What's funny?' she says.

'My father always says that a liar glances up before he speaks. I wasn't cruising. I came here looking for you.'

She sweeps a sprinkling of snow from the log which I realise with a shock is the one where I'd put the body of the dead bird.

'You can sit down if you want,' she says.

I ski over and awkwardly sit down down next to her. Our bodies are squashed together with our legs touching but neither of us wriggles apart. This is a good sign and suddenly I feel emboldened. I remove my gloves then take her hand. I've never felt anything as soft and lovely as her skin. It's like being touched by a cloud. Shivers run up my arm and make the hairs prickle. I reach into my pocket, take out the five hundred dollars and place it in her palm.

'For you,' I say.

She holds the notes and stares at them. What's she thinking now?

'For the Somali children,' she finally says with just the hint of a smile.

'For them as well,' I say.

She doesn't speak. I feel like a person in a dream who is walking down the street naked. She seems to see right into me. Finally she says, 'The children are coming on the fifteenth.'

'My birthday,' I say.

'They're the ones who are getting the present,' she says. 'It's incredibly kind of you, Robin, and the kids will all have a wonderful holiday. If the money was just for me, I couldn't accept it. Thank you so much.'

'No worries,' I say.

But I do have worries. I'm elated that I've pleased her. I'm happy the Somali kids will get their trip. But if I examine my motives, I know that it wasn't totally idealism that led me to donate so much money. Would I have put my hand up for any other girl? Of course not – I wouldn't have done it for *anyone* else. So does this make the whole deed nothing but selfish?

'I can't believe that stingy mob at school,' she says. 'The teachers were good but hardly anyone else contributed.'

I wonder if I can kiss her now. 'I'm sorry for running off that night,' I say. 'I was an idiot.'

'It doesn't matter. You must have had your reasons.'

'I did. The balaclava had my father's spit on it.'

'Oh, yuck! But why did that make you run? I thought you hated me when you disappeared like that.'

'Hated you? No way. Just the opposite.'

'So, why did you run off?'

I don't know if I can tell her. This is big. 'I got an image.'

'What do you mean you got an image? What sort of image?'

'A picture in my head.'

'Like what?'

'Like a flashing photo of something real happening. Or a cork popping. Horrible. The worst thing.'

'I don't get it. A popping cork's fun.'

'No, it's awful. I see myself doing something terrible and then I freak out because it's the opposite of what I would ever want to do. It's nearly always something to do with my father.'

'But isn't that normal?'

'No – it's too terrible to . . .' I hesitate. This is getting dangerous. I don't want to tell her about this.

I'm saved when something moves on the ground near Charlie's feet. It flutters.

The blood runs backwards in my veins. The world spins in reverse. It's the blue wren. Its wings flap. The poor thing's still suffering. It didn't die when I put it in the icy water. It's been in agony all this time. Oh no, I can't believe it. I have to end its pain. Quick.

I drop to the ground, take hold of the tiny creature and close my eyes. There's a click as I twist the bird's neck.

Charlie gapes at me in shock and leaps up from the log. 'What are you doing?' she shouts. 'Killing a poor little bird.' Her face is contorted into a horrified stare.

Black nightmares dance inside my head. I search

for words to explain. 'It's not what you think,' I gasp, looking up at her desperately.

'Don't talk to me,' she says. 'I don't want to know what you think.' She picks up her skis and runs down the darkening track like a wounded deer lifting its feet high as it struggles through the snow.

'Come back,' I call.

She plunges on and disappears into the trees, not giving me a chance to explain. She hung the death of the bird around my neck, leaving me standing there hopelessly calling for her to come back.

I'm left alone in the cold forest with my thoughts.

After the weekend it's back to school. I try to talk to Charlie on the bus but she's listening to her ipod and ignores me. I notice Verushka watching me and realise that she's seen it all. I'm expecting her to smirk but instead she smiles in a friendly way which is unusual for her. It washes away just a tiny bit of my gloom.

I go searching for Charlie in the lunchbreak but she spends the whole time hanging around with a group of girls. She wears her friends like armour and there's no way I can get near her for a private conversation. On the bus she sits right up the front with Laura and Janie where she knows she'll be safe. Halfway up the mountain I kick myself for not texting her while we were still in range. I don't want to ring her landline because her parents might listen.

All that week it's the same and I come to the conclusion that I'll be in trouble for harassment if I persist; they're big on that sort of thing at Bright Dale School. She's not even giving me a chance to explain so I make one last attempt and send her a short email saying: *Can I talk to you?*

Her reply comes straight back: *I'm not opening your emails. Please leave me alone. I'd give your rotten money back if I could but it's already gone to the organisers.*

I feel angry but try to put myself in her situation. I'll have to leave her alone after this but on Friday, after

Dad's gone to bed, I send a final email. In the subject bar I write: *Please read this, Charlie.*

The email is the hardest thing I've ever written. I go over and over it deleting words and adding phrases, explaining how I'd tried to be merciful to the little bird and how hard it was for me to end its agony by breaking its neck. I read over the email one last time and then hesitate with the cursor hovering over the *send* button. Is my message good enough? No, it will never be good enough but it's the best I can do. I click the mouse and the message is gone.

I throw myself on the bed and stare out of the window. Five minutes later I jump at the ding of a message arriving in my Inbox. I dart over to the computer and read Charlie's reply: *Leave me alone. I'm deleting your messages without opening them.*

So that's that. For the next month I avoid anywhere I know Charlie might be hanging out. She's doing the same. I tell myself that she's not worth worrying about but that's a joke because I can't stop thinking about her. Gradually I start to wonder why I'm being so stubborn.

By the time my birthday arrives I'm feeling hopeful. The Somali children will be on the slopes and Charlie will be with them for sure. I'll go and look for her; after all they wouldn't even be here if it wasn't for my donation. Maybe something good will happen.

'Happy birthday,' says Dad at breakfast as he hands me his gift. I can see right away what it is because he hasn't wrapped it. 'Wrapping paper is a waste of money,' he says. 'In ten seconds it's ripped and useless.'

'You're right,' I say, looking at the icepick before me.

'It'll be useful if you get lost in the snow. You could use it to dig yourself a cave until help comes. And when you're not using it I can borrow it when I have to go and rescue some idiot who's broken down on a snowmobile.'

He senses that I'm not jumping with joy over his present. 'I've gone to a lot of trouble to customise it, you know,' he says, his voice rising half an octave. 'I've put that steel loop on the handle to attach a rope to in emergencies. You could lower yourself down a cliff if you were stuck. Or use it to climb back up out of a crevasse. I've sharpened the point to give it better grip. So don't tell me I don't care about you. Everything I do is for you.'

'Thanks, Dad.'

I run my thumb over the tip of the pointy end of the icepick. It's like a needle. I shudder, and put it down. A snake strikes before I can run and I grimace as the image hits me. It only lasts for a split second but the knowledge that I'm a person who can let a hideous vision into my mind lingers like the ache of poison after the snake has struck.

'I'll hang it with the other tools,' I say. I gingerly pick up the icepick by its pointy end.

'Speaking of tools,' he says, completely unaware of what I've just been going through, 'we've got a lot of repairs today.'

'It's my birthday, Dad! Remember? You said I could have the day off.'

'Damn it,' he says. 'Can't you make it another day?'

'You promised.'

'I know, I know. It's your birthday. Be selfish then. Off you go. Don't worry about me. Enjoy yourself.'

I leave the workshop while I've got the chance and try not to feel guilty about it.

It's a busy day on the slopes. We've had good falls of snow and now the weather is clear – just what the tourists love. Further down the hill, the parking bays are full of snow-covered cars and buses lined up like giant loaves of bread.

It's going to be hard to find Charlie amongst the crowds already spilling down the runs. I cross under the chairlift and search the slopes hoping to catch a glimpse of her. No luck. I glide down to the poma and see some tall black kids having fun on the learners' slope. They are accompanied by a few adults – and Charlie, wearing her red parka. Some of the girls are laughing and falling over as they practise snowplough turns. Charlie leads one of the girls to the poma. The poles dangle down from the moving cable like long inverted bar stools and bounce up and down on their connecting springs as they clank their way uphill. Charlie's girl moves slowly forward waiting her turn in the line. She watches as one by one the skiers put a poma pole between their legs and shove the dinner-plate disc behind their bum. It looks easy, just standing there letting yourself be pulled up the hill on a platter tow, but it isn't.

'Don't sit down, Nadia,' says Charlie.

I know that Nadia's going to sit down. Everyone does the first time. Sure enough Nadia grabs the pole, shoves it between her legs and puts all her weight onto the disc. The spring stretches and she drops onto her backside in the snow with a thump. For a frozen moment she just sits there then she desperately clings to the pole as the spring begins to stretch and she's dragged along like a bundle of old rags. Finally she lets go and the whole thing snaps away from her with a clang. She rolls to one side and looks up, confused but unhurt. Everyone laughs, including me.

Charlie sees me and turns away. She's not going to

talk to me, but she bends down and speaks to Nadia who takes off her skis and walks clumsily towards me in her ski boots. She gives a nervous smile with teeth that are whiter than the snow.

'Thank you for bringing us here,' she says shyly and without waiting for an answer she turns away. She takes a few steps then turns back. 'Happy birthday.'

I smile and watch her hurry over to the group. So Charlie *has* remembered it's my birthday. She must still like me a bit. I begin to follow Nadia but Charlie shakes her head with a frown.

It's like a knife in my guts.

Another week passes. My whole body and mind are tuned to Charlie. Something is missing and I can't function properly. It's as if someone has taken away one of my vital organs. I keep making mistakes in the workshop. I over-tightened three nuts on the studs of a cylinder head and stripped the threads. The old man was not amused because we didn't have a stud puller and it took ages to get the ruined studs out. Then I dropped the spirit level and broke the glass in it. Of course I never heard the end of that.

I constantly look out of the open workshop doors hoping I will see Charlie ski past. Every time I see a girl in a red parka my heart jumps.

'Stop dreaming,' says Dad. 'Concentrate. Time is money.'

I decide to write Charlie a letter – I have to end this torture. She might not read it, but at least I'll have done all I can, and who knows, maybe one day she will, and then she'll understand.

I sit down at my computer and start tapping out my explanation. I write it out exactly the way it happened, making it clear that I'd already tried to put the wren out of its misery in the kindest way I could, and telling her how much I want to be her friend – which is putting it mildly but, hey, one step at a time.

The next morning, which is Saturday, I put on my old leather jacket and trudge across the ski slope on legs that wobble with emotion. I knock on Charlie's door and it's answered by Russell.

'Hi, Russell,' I say. 'Sorry to bother you but is Charlie in?' I look over his shoulder in case she comes to see who's at the door but the only thing that comes out is a delicious smell of hot bread from the kitchen.

'Yes, she's home,' he says. 'But I'm sorry, Robin, she doesn't want to see you.'

'She's been avoiding me for ages,' I say. 'Something happened and she misunderstood. Will you give her this letter, please?'

He takes the envelope from me. 'I don't know what happened between you two, Robin, but I know Charlie. You'll have to respect her wishes. I'll give it to her, but if she throws it out unread you'll just have to live with it.'

'Thanks, Russell. See you.' Suddenly I feel incredibly desolate, and for a moment I think about telling him everything. After all, he understands why it's sometimes necessary to put animals down. But then I think maybe Charlie has told him about the way I ran off after dinner.

They're really close so she might have. I can't lie to him and I can't tell him *why* I ran either – no one must ever know. I nearly told Charlie.

But I was saved by the bird.

# The Torch

Ho, yuss, there be a tiger named Tiger in this story. In the forest. Of the night.

Ho, yuss, there be a duck named Verity in this story. In the forest. Of the night.

Ho, yuss, there be a man named Gordon in this story. In the forest. Of the night.

I don't know why I am talking like this. It just seems like the thing to do. Anyway, to get down to the tale, or maybe to the tail, it goes like this:

A poor man lived in the jungle in a little hut. He had a major problem. He was so scared of the dark that he would never go out at night. Not only that, he would never – not ever – turn out the light. It was almost as if the darkness was acid rain that might fall down and smother him. The hut had but one door and no windows.

Every night the man slept with the light on and kept the door tightly closed from dusk till dawn. Even when the moon was bright, he was too frightened to venture out in case it went behind a cloud. Without the moon he was dead.

Ho, yuss.

No woman would live with this man because he was afraid of the dark. So he dwelt with a white duck instead. Verity, the duck, waddled around in the hut as if she owned it. She sat on the chairs and did white poo. She sat on the table and did white poo. She sat on the bed and did white poo. She sat on the ceiling light and did white poo. The whole of the inside of the hut was covered in the stuff. It was dreadful. But it was not dark inside the hut. Everything was white. Duck-poo white. It sparkled in the bright beam of the ceiling light.

The man loved the duck. She was his friend, his mate, his life (but not his wife). Without the duck he would die of loneliness. The man knew that.

Ho, yuss.

Outside in the jungle the tiger roamed by day but not by night. Tiger was fearsome and terrible. He had yellow and black stripes and could not be seen in the dense foliage. When the tiger growled it was like the noise the bath makes when the plug is pulled, only a hundred times louder. If anyone were to see this tiger it would be the last thing they would see. He was a fearsome tiger.

Oh, and I forgot to say:

Ho, yuss, there be a Prince of Darkness in this story. He was scared of the dark too, but he loved to shine it on others.

I am going to call him the POD because Prince of Darkness is too long a phrase to keep typing out. The man was terrified of the POD because of his fearsome torch.

This torch worked in the day – yes, the day. In the full light of the sun it cast its darkness. Yes, darkness. It shone rays blacker than the blackest night. The POD could shine (if that's the word) the torch across a sunlit field. A black, black beam would cut through the sparkling sunshine. Everything it fell upon would vanish into its shadow.

One day as the man stood at his door looking through the forest clearing he saw the POD creep up behind Verity, the duck. Tiger was sitting on the branch of a low tree. *Click.* The POD switched on his terrible torch. The black beam engulfed the duck.

She disappeared from sight.

'Oh, no,' cried the man. He wanted to rush out and save the duck but he was frightened that the deadly torch would be turned upon him. The POD chuckled and laughed in a wicked way. Then he switched off the torch. The poor duck sat there stunned. She was now a black duck. All her feathers were singed and burnt. She said, 'Quack.'

Ho, yuss.

Next the POD crept up behind the tiger who was warming himself in the sun. *Click.* The POD switched on the black beam. The tiger was engulfed in darkness. The POD chuckled his evil chuckle and after he had finished with the chuckling he turned off his torch. The tiger's black stripes were blacker than before. His yellow stripes were gone altogether. His whole coat was burnt and singed. The tiger was fearsome no more. He opened his mouth and made a very tiny bath-plug noise.

Now the POD turned his attention to the shaking man who backed into the hut and slammed the door. The handle turned. The POD entered clutching his evil torch. The man eyed the open door and looked for his chance to escape. But the POD closed the door behind him and leant on it. There was no exit. The POD pointed the torch of darkness at the shaking man. His thumb moved towards the switch.

*Click.*

The room was cast into darkness. The whole room. The POD screamed. It was not his click. The man had beaten him to it. He had switched off the ceiling light. He had chosen to put himself into the darkness.

There was another click and then another scream from the POD. His black beam could not shine in the darkness. He was now engulfed in his own nightmare.

In the blackness the man saw many sights. Heard many sounds. Felt many feels. He froze and burnt and was blown in the wind. He plummeted to the depths. He soared to the heights. He crashed to the floor.

Finally he crawled to the door of the hut and out into the blinding light of day. The POD, who for the first time had experienced his own black nightmare, staggered out and fled naked and smoking across the field.

The duck and the tiger and the man watched him go.

The tiger was now a black panther. He rather liked it. He stood on his hind legs and began to jig and jog. The duck flapped and cavorted with him. The man joined them and together they danced the day away.

That next day the man cleaned out the duck poo. In the coming months he made a pond for the duck and found himself a wife. He was burnt and singed and totally bald for the rest of his life. But he was never frightened of the dark again.

That is my tale. If you ask me what it means I will say nothing at all.

I made it up.

Ho, yuss.

# THE NEST

3

Some days nothing goes right from the time you get out of bed until the time you get back in again at night. I'm making toast for breakfast and a slice gets stuck in the toaster which I start trying to fish out with a knife.

Dad snatches the knife from my hand. 'Idiot,' he hisses. 'You haven't even turned the power off.'

'Sorry.'

He shakes his head, letting me know he really does think I'm hopeless. And I am.

'Go clean the spark plug on that snowmobile

Mountain Rescue brought in. I'll be there in a minute.'

'Where's the spark-plug spanner?' I ask when his tall frame casts its shadow through the workshop door.

He looks at the rack and sees that it's not in its place. 'I *told* you to clean up. You'd forget your head if it wasn't screwed on,' he says, fishing the spanner out of his pocket and throwing it at me.

'Sorry, Dad,' I say.

He suddenly notices the nest up on the wall just inside the door. 'Didn't I ask you to get rid of that bloody thing? The filthy birds will be back again come spring.'

Swallows' droppings run down the wall like food on a baby's bib. I just hadn't been able to bring myself to destroy the nest, not after what happened in the forest.

'I forgot,' I say.

'Liar.'

His face turns white and his anger grows like a snowball rolling down a hill. Little gobs of spit form a rim around his mouth. 'Robin, every day I slave in this workshop. I'm father *and* mother. I get lonely, you know. I get tired, but I don't forget about you. What about me? Why do you forget about me?'

'Sorry,' I say again. 'I've got a few things on my mind.'

'Get rid of the bloody thing before tomorrow,' he says.

'Okay, I will.' I go over to the snowmobile and disconnect the high-tension lead which I hold in my left hand.

'Put your other hand on the spark plug,' says Dad.

I follow his orders automatically and he twists the starter key and turns over the engine. A million tiny jackhammers suddenly drill into every organ in my body. My teeth eat at each other and my jaw goes into a crazy dance. It's like an army of dentists' drills at work on every centimetre of bone and flesh. I'm under attack from within. It's an implosion of blunt hailstones.

He takes out the key and the pain stops as quickly as it began. I shake in the aftermath of the shock.

'That'll teach you to respect electricity,' he says.

On the bench is the icepick. Instantly I get an image of jabbing him with it right in the middle of his bald patch. A cerebral snake has bitten me. I have to run. I have to get out of here. I storm out of the workshop and rush to my room where I curl up into a ball on the bed. What Dad did was cruel but the image that flashed into my mind was something worse. I try to figure it out. I didn't want to kill him. I didn't want the image. Causing pain is evil and I would never do it.

Or would I? Is there something dark and terrible lurking inside me that isn't in anyone else? *Could* I lose control and commit murder?

I try to distract myself by pulling out the bottom drawer of my dressing-table and taking out my mother's hairbrush. I slowly brush my hair with it. Some of my own black hair catches in the bristles and becomes entwined with the few red strands of hers. It's a sign, but of what I don't know. I start to feel better. I decide to go for a walk and see if the fresh air can clear my mind.

The workshop is deserted. Dad's nowhere around.

I'm just by the door when I hear a voice. 'Hi, Robin.'

I look up. 'Hi.' It's Verushka.

She peers at me through those half-closed eyes. 'Feel like a coffee?' she says. 'You look like you need one.'

I'm still quivering a little but I manage to answer and sound relaxed. 'Sure,' I say, wondering what she really wants. 'Come on in.'

'Not here, dummy, let's go to Candleglow.'

Now I'm intrigued. 'Okay, I'll just clean up a bit.'

I wash my hands in the old sink and take my jacket from the hook on the workshop door. Dad isn't going to complain about my absence this time. It's like when he threw Mum's ring out: he knows he did wrong but he'll never admit it, so he goes silent and gives off vibes that tell me quite clearly the incident can never be mentioned.

Verushka and I walk slowly across the ski slope. I've never seen her skiing. She always walks everywhere even though she lives in a ski village. We get to the café and it's pretty crowded but there are a few tables free. I drop into a seat.

'Not there, dummy,' says Verushka. 'It's noisy. The best tables are by the window. You can keep an eye on what's going on.'

We move to a table where we can see clear across the valley to the mountains beyond. The snow-capped peaks are like rows of sharks' teeth.

'I'll get the coffees,' I say.

'A latte and a slice of mudcake,' says Verushka.

I make my way over to the counter and place our order. When I get back I see that she's peeled off her parka to reveal a really low-cut top which I try hard not to stare at. I take off my jacket and hang it on the back of the chair.

'God, you're ready for a new coat,' she says, looking at the worn leather sleeves. 'But then I guess you won't have much money left for clothes after your big gesture.'

I feel my face turning red. 'Huh?' I say, pretending not to understand.

'You know what I'm talking about. I heard you're not too popular with Charlie these days. What happened?'

She stares at me intently from beneath her long fringe.

'Oh, it's just one of those things,' I say, trying to look casual about it. 'You know how it is.'

'No I don't, actually. The word is that she's not speaking to you.'

'Well, I don't speak to her either.'

'Why not?' she persists.

'A misunderstanding. Forget it.'

'Don't you miss her?'

'Nup.'

'I'll hang out with you if you like,' she says.

I'm surprised. It's always been her and Ryan. But on the other hand, she *has* seemed to stare at me a lot lately. I search around for a reply but the coffees arrive and save me the trouble.

'You can be my slave,' she continues once we're alone again.

'What?'

'It'll be fun.'

I just stare at her, trying not to look astonished.

'You can sit with me on the bus after school and then carry my bag back here when we arrive and we'll have coffee together.'

'Are you serious?' I think she's making fun of me.

She laughs and stirs her latte. It's almost a childish laugh, as if she's been given a toy.

'What about Ryan?' I say.

'I'm not talking to him.'

'Why not?'

She throws my words back at me, mockingly. 'Oh, it's just one of those things. You know how it is.'

'Right,' I say and then add, 'I thought you liked him.'

'I used to, but he's started to annoy me. He's getting on my nerves. He's such a child. Gets upset about nothing.'

'Like what?' I ask, but she just gives me a look that says 'don't go there'.

She's even weirder than I thought. Be her slave? I'm slave enough already, thanks very much. The old man – hey, stop thinking about him. Being a slave to a sexy girl might be something else altogether.

Right at that moment I see Charlie glide down the slope outside. She has perfect balance on her skis. God, she's lovely, but she doesn't care about me – she just took the money and ran.

'Well,' says Verushka. 'What about it?'

'I'll tell you tomorrow,' I say, stalling for time. It's a big step to hang out with Verushka.

'Suit yourself,' she says getting up and leaving her mudcake untouched on the table.

I watch her walk unhurriedly across the café and leave. She's a strange girl all right.

The woman who owns the Polar Bare nightclub is supposed to be Verushka's guardian while her parents are overseas but as far as I can make out there's not much guarding going on. Verushka has moved into the youth hostel and seems to do whatever she pleases. Behind those half-closed eyes there's danger and adventure and who knows what?

I make up my mind.

I'll do it.

On Monday I wait for Verushka at the bus stop in the dark of the winter morning. Soon the bus will come to take us down the mountain with the scattering of other kids who live on the ski slope. Most of their parents work on the tows or in the cafés or the ski-hire shops or other businesses in the village.

Verushka appears out of the mist and glides slowly towards me. I open my mouth to speak but she hands me her pack without a word and climbs into the bus. I pass Charlie as we make our way along the aisle but she doesn't even look up.

After school I wait by the bus for the return trip. Verushka makes for where I'm standing and hands over her backpack. She sleeps all the way home, and in the Candleglow confides that she hates it here in the mountains. Because I'm the one with the part-time job I pay for our coffees. She tells me that on Saturday nights she often goes to the Polar Bare. She's a year older than me but she's still not really old enough for nightclubs. She gets in because she mixes with the ski instructors and knows the guys on the door as well as the owner who obviously turns a blind eye.

I've never known anyone like Verushka. People probably think she's my girlfriend when they see us sitting together but she makes it clear I'm not.

'It's just platonic, Robin,' she says.

I wish it was more than platonic but it's better than nothing. We say goodbye at the café and I don't get to go to her place.

This becomes our daily ritual. One day, after about a week, Verushka is especially animated as we board the morning bus. 'This is the last time I make this lousy trip to school,' she says gleefully.

My heart sinks. 'How come?'

'Wait till we sit down.'

We go to our usual spot and she gives me the news. 'I've got a job at the Polar Bare. Behind the bar.'

'You can't have. It's illegal. You're not eighteen yet!'

She gives me a wink and taps the side of her nose with one finger. 'Don't look so miserable, dummy,' she says. 'You can still meet me – after art class. I'll be getting Wednesdays off so I'll be going to town for shopping and then the class in the evening. You can meet me after school and then work in the library while I'm at class. We'll catch the late bus back up the mountain.'

'Doesn't Ryan go to art classes?'

'So?' She gives me another one of those 'don't go there' looks.

For the next couple of weeks, on Wednesday nights, I meet Verushka before and after art class. The old man kicked up about me catching the late bus back but when I told him I was staying to work in the library he let it go. Verushka and I hang out together after school, then I catch up with homework while I wait to pick her up at eight o'clock. If Ryan sees me on his way out of class, he just scowls and looks the other way. On the bus home, Verushka and I talk about all sorts of things including her plans to own her own nightclub one day. She's also interested in my stories and has read a couple. She says I've got talent and this makes me blush.

One Wednesday after school I can see she has

something to tell me. She often gets a cheeky expression when something quite trivial has taken her interest. It's sort of cute – I think. I wonder what it is this time.

'For you,' she says. She reaches into her pack and pulls out a beautifully wrapped present. It has blue ribbon neatly tied around red wrapping paper, finishing in a stylish bow.

I'm taken aback. Perhaps our relationship is moving up to a new level.

'It's not new,' she says. 'But I want you to have it.'

I pull off the ribbon and open the package. It's a paperback book called *How to be Cool*.

I flip through the pages. The book is all about what's hot – what sort of haircut is in, what the best styles are and stuff like that. I feel a bit insulted and don't know what to say except 'thanks'.

'That's okay,' she replies. 'You need a new image. You're good looking but your clothes let you down. And your hair.'

I'd really never thought much about these things

before. I guess she's right. I need to keep up with the guys in the Polar Bare if I want to continue seeing Verushka.

'Come on,' she says. 'I'm taking you shopping. We'll start with those old boots. The guys in the Polar Bare are into pointy shoes. They look fabulous.'

Verushka leads me to an expensive designer shop where she helps me pick out a new pair. They're Italian. Black. Very soft leather. As I hand over the money to the guy in the store I make a mental note that I had to work three weekends in the workshop with the old man to get it.

'Worth every cent,' says Verushka admiringly.

I keep the new shoes on and head back to wait in the library feeling sort of pleased but also worried. I always seem to end up doing what Verushka wants. I hardly know anything about her. Still, she must care about me to take all this interest so I decide to chance it and push things a bit. I arrive at the old hall which is now an art studio and hang about by the front door, with only the moon for company. The first one out is Ryan.

His step falters as he sees me but he recovers, sneers and disappears into the night. Finally, everyone in the class except Verushka has packed up and left. The last person out has to lock up and tonight it's her.

'I want to see one of your paintings,' I tell her just as she's about to put the key in the door. 'It's only fair. You've read some of my stories. I want to see what you do.'

At first she gives me one of her warning looks, but then she nods and without a word opens the door and beckons me in. It's still warm inside and there's a strong smell of turps. There are empty easels and trays of paint and one long, splattered wooden table. Lockers stand against the walls and half-finished paintings lean wonkily in their racks. A Chinese silk dressing-gown is draped over a chair in the middle of the room.

Verushka points to the canvases. 'Pick one out then,' she says. 'Any one.'

'I want to see yours,' I say.

She doesn't reply but glares at me. This means 'don't argue'.

I do as she says and we both look at the painting I've

chosen. It's of a young woman sitting on a dragon and has been done in a sort of modern airbrushed style that could have sprung from the cover of a science-fiction book. The colours are garish and shiny. The woman has a brilliant sari wrapped around her waist but wears nothing else. Her breasts are totally exposed. She has sleepy, knowing eyes.

'It's you,' I yelp.

Verushka lifts out another painting which is also of her. It's cubist or whatever they call it and you can only tell it's her by the eyes that are painted stacked on top of each other. She takes out another piece which only shows her from the waist up giving the impression that she's totally naked. Her breasts seem huge and . . . incredible. I can hardly believe that I'm looking at them. The artist has painted a stylish watch on her arm and underneath has written: *Good-Time Girl*. Verushka takes out three more canvases in quick succession and drops them back against the wall after waving each one in my face. Her breasts are revealed in all of them.

I'm astounded.

She's laughing now. 'I can't paint for nuts,' she says. 'I'm a model, you silly.'

'How can you do it?' I say in a shocked voice.

'You don't have to worry,' she says. 'The place is heated. I don't get cold.'

'I don't mean *that*,' I shout. 'They all see you half naked. Why do you do it?' I feel wave after wave of disappointment and anger sweep over me.

'Money, of course. What do you think? It's well paid. How else am I going to get off the mountain? Barmaids don't get much. If it wasn't for the tips I'd never save anything.'

'Who did the one with the watch?' I say, already knowing the answer.

'Ryan did.'

'It's disgusting,' I yell.

'Don't be a baby,' she says. 'You're jealous.'

'I don't like him painting you like . . . like that.'

Her face contorts with fury. 'You are so childish,' she screams. 'You don't know anything.'

She fumbles at the zip of her parka and rips it down towards her navel. Before I can even register what she's doing, the parka is on the floor and she's peeling off her thick jumper and a thin top beneath it. She tears at her bra and I hear the rip of torn stitching. She tosses the dead garment into the air. 'Here,' she says scornfully. 'This is what you want.'

She's right. It *is* what I want. She is beautiful. She is terrible. She is awesome. What the hell. What does it matter if she offers herself with a taunt? I feel myself take a step forward and as I do, I catch a glimpse of the silk dressing-gown, the one that only a short time ago she carelessly removed to reveal herself to other eyes. Hidden inside the black curse of jealousy is a tiny grain of self-respect which makes me hesitate.

'Get someone else to be your slave,' I yell as I burst out into the cold night.

The bus trip back up the mountain seems to last for ever. Verushka sits in her usual seat and I stretch out at the back, pretending I'm asleep. I'm filled with lust and loathing.

The bus is heated. But the atmosphere is cold. Freezing cold.

Two days pass. I awake in my bedroom to find that the window is glazed with frost. Wonderful patterns are illuminated by the ski-slope lights which are always turned on before dawn to allow the snow to be groomed. In one corner of the window the cold breath of the night has painted a picture that looks like a woman's face. I let my imagination roam. It's my mother. I know it is. The misty woman can sense my sorrow. I trace her gently with my finger and she begins to melt into tears which run slowly down the glass.

She's gone.

I take Mum's hairbrush out of the hiding place under my bottom drawer and let its gentle aura wash over me. I gently touch the few long red hairs entwined in the bristles and imagine Mum using it. It's time to get up but I drift off to sleep thinking of how much I'd love to know her. One day I'll find her, I know I will.

I'm suddenly awakened by a distant rasping voice. 'Get a move on, Robin, or you'll miss the bloody bus.' The old man is yelling at me from somewhere down below. The sound sets my nerves on edge.

I dress and rush off without stopping for breakfast or saying goodbye. Now I'm feeling really cranky. It's not a good start to the last day of term and I have a premonition that it's going to get worse.

And I'm not wrong. Halfway through second period I'm summoned to the principal's office. You have to sit outside his door where everyone who passes wonders why you're there. That's one thing *I* don't need to wonder about. I've got a pretty good idea what he wants. I sit there acting like I'm unconcerned. After about fifteen minutes his secretary tells me I can go in.

Mr Henderson is one of those people who doesn't believe in talking to you from behind a desk. He stands up and points to two small lounge chairs which face each other over a coffee table. He's not a bad guy but if you cross him he can give you a hard time. He throws a story I have written onto the table and gives me a reproachful look.

'Frankly, it's disgusting, Robin,' he says indicating the pages of my manuscript.

'What's wrong with it, Mr Henderson?' I say, trying to sound innocent.

'You know very well what's wrong with it. If something like this gets out to the local paper we'll be in all sorts of strife. Mrs Zeigler asked your Creative Writing class to write a children's story and you come up with this which is definitely *not* a children's story.'

'In one way it is,' I say.

'Come on, no parent would let their child read this. How does it fit the definition?'

'It's written by a child so it's a child's book.'

'You're drawing a long bow there, Robin. It's meant to be *for* a child. Not *by* a child. And anyway, you're sixteen. You're not a child anymore.'

'But I'm still *treated* like a child,' I say, warming to my theme. 'I can't vote. I can't drink and I can't drive. I even have to put my hand up to get permission to go to the toilet. So this is a child's story because it was written by a child. I'm a person who sees things from a different point of view.'

'Don't give me that, Robin. Just because you know where to put a possessive apostrophe doesn't mean that you can make a monkey out of one of my teachers. I don't mind people seeing things from a different point of view but you're stretching things too far.' He waves a piece of paper at me. 'Some principals would suspend you for this. Or contact your parents.'

On the wall above his head is a photograph of the snow-covered ski village on the mountain. I can see my father's workshop downhill from the chairlift. The doors are open and there's a little smudge which just might be him. Inside my head a snake strikes. I can't stay here.

'I have to go,' I say pushing the chair back to get up.

'I'm not finished,' he says.

I stand. 'Sorry,' I say, 'but I can't stay.' My voice is rising in panic.

'You're not going anywhere until we've resolved this,' he says.

I take a few steps. He speaks to my back. 'I'll be in contact with your mo–' He catches himself just in time.

I turn and face him. 'I haven't got a mother.'

'Yes, I'm sorry, Robin. I meant your father.'

He feels bad and speaks less harshly. He picks up my manuscript and starts to flip over the pages. He's skim-reading it. I don't think he's even read it properly. He just accepted what Mrs Zeigler said.

'You were only a baby, Robin. It's not your fault your mother left.'

'Apparently it was,' I say.

'Is that what you think?'

'It's what my father says.'

His voice is gentle now as he casts his eyes down the last page. He starts tapping the pages with his index finger. 'Some things aren't always black and white. There may be more to it than you think. Have you made enquiries as to where she might have gone?'

'Dad won't tell me anything.'

'I mean through official channels.'

'Dad would freak out,' I say. Mr Henderson's words, 'not your fault', are like the menace of a rattler's warning.

'Robin, you seem very upset, so I'd like you to make an appointment with Mr Rogers,' he says. 'Preferably this afternoon.'

I don't answer. Mr Rogers is the school counsellor and he'll try to get inside my head. I can't let anyone in. Ever.

Aaagh. Another snake bites me. 'Sorry, I have to go.'

'Come back here, Robin.'

I open the door. 'I can't stay,' I say.

'I *will* have to contact your father.'

'He'll make things worse,' I shout as I run out of his office.

The aftershock of the images lingers as I head back to class.

# The Tree

Once upon a time, there was a bunch of weird trees living in a forest. They were snow gums and every winter the poor bloody things were covered in snow. In spring birds would nest in their hair.

Grandmother Tree was crotchety because hairy caterpillars were crawling all over her and eating the leaves on her twigs again.

Little Jack was cracking the sads because dogs were pissing on his trunk again.

'It sucks being a tree,' said Father Tree. 'We just have to stand here and cop all this shit.'

'I know,' said Mother Tree. 'But don't swear in front of Little Jack, dear.'

'Why couldn't the world be made with no frigging birds?' said Father Tree.

'Or caterpillars?' said Mother Tree, giving him a frown for swearing again.

'Or dogs?' said Little Jack. 'Their piss really stinks and you can't get it off.'

Suddenly Little Jack saw something growing near by. 'Look,' he said.

They all stared. They were over the moon.

'We're having a baby,' said Mother Tree.

'I didn't know you two had been at it again,' said Little Jack.

'It's a boy,' said Mother Tree giving another frown.

'A son,' said Dad.

'We'll call him Gordon,' said Mother Tree.

In only two years, Gordon had grown tall and strong. One day Mother Tree and Dad saw him doing something odd.

'No,' yelled Dad.

'No, no,' yelled Mother Tree.

'No, no, no,' yelled Little Jack.

'What?' said Gordon. 'What's the matter?'

'You're moving your branches,' said Grandmother Tree. 'It's not allowed.'

'Only the wind should bend your branches,' said Dad.

'It's not natural to do it yourself,' said Grandfather Tree.

'The boy's peculiar,' said Dad.

'He can shoo off the bloody birds with his branches, though,' said Little Jack. 'That's cool. That's really cool.'

'And he can pick off the horrible caterpillars,' said Grandmother Tree.

'And piss off the bloody dogs,' said Little Jack. 'That's far out.'

'No,' said Father Tree. 'We just have to put up with birds and caterpillars and dogs. Trees have to stand and take it.'

'Now look at him,' said Little Jack.

'Gordon,' shouted Dad. 'How dare you. Don't do that.'

Grandmother Tree closed her eyes in shame.

Gordon was rubbing a short twig that had been pruned when he was just a baby.

'He's wanking!' yelled Little Jack.

After that, no one in the forest wanted to talk to poor Gordon. Only Mother Tree and Little Jack.

Dad and Mother Tree began to argue about what Gordon was doing. Every day they would argue.

'Leave him alone,' said Mother Tree.

'He's an idiot,' said Dad. 'Totally loopy, out of his tree.'

'Don't call him an idiot,' said Mother Tree.

'You're an idiot too,' said Dad.

'Don't speak to me like that,' said Mother Tree.

'Be quiet, woman,' ordered Dad.

Mother Tree could take no more. 'This arguing is all too much for me,' she said. She began to scratch at the dirt.

'What are you doing?' yelled Father Tree. 'That's against the rules.'

'Digging,' she said.

'Stop at once, you fool,' said Father Tree. 'You are a tree, not a rabbit.'

Mother Tree did not stop. She dug around her roots with her twigs.

All the trees in the forest were horrified.

Mother Tree stepped out of her hole.

'Now what are you doing?' screamed Dad.

'Running away,' she said.

'Get back in your hole,' said Father Tree. 'At once.'

Mother Tree did not get back into her hole. She was sick of Father Tree's bullying.

She walked off over the hill. And never came back.

Father Tree was angry. He yelled at Gordon. 'It's all your fault.'

A sudden thought came into Gordon's consciousness. He saw himself reaching over and ripping every leaf off his father's head. But it was just an image that flitted into his mind like the wind passing through dry grass.

He didn't really want to do it. It was just a thought.

# THE NEST

## 4

After I leave the principal's office I go back to my Maths class. I'm not going to make an appointment with Mr Rogers. Kids who go there are either psychos or misfits and I'm neither. Or maybe I'm both. Either way I'm not having any labels hung around my neck.

I go through every class on automatic. I do what I have to do but I don't join in discussions or answer questions. I sit up the back thinking about the way my life is going down the gurgler. When the final bell sounds I grab my bag and make my escape.

The bus isn't there. Now we'll all be late getting home, which is a pain when everyone wants to get away for the school holidays. The bus kids start to mill around on the footpath. I don't feel like talking to anyone so I go back inside the school gate and sit on the edge of the fountain. It hasn't been turned on in two years because of the water restrictions. I sit there and think.

A shadow blots out the sun. I look up but at first I can't make out who it is because he's silhouetted against the bright light.

'Hi, Robin,' says Mr Rogers.

'Hi, Mr Rogers,' I say with a resigned sigh. He doesn't look like a teacher with his faded jeans, T-shirt and denim jacket. He's not a bad bloke – one of the most popular staff members actually – but if you go to see him everyone knows about it. Already I can see a couple of kids looking over in our direction. I thought I saw Charlie glancing my way but maybe it was just my imagination.

Mr Henderson's obviously told Mr Rogers I've got a problem, and he's come looking for me. I'm wary; there's no way I'm going to start blabbing about my flickering images.

'Call me Steve,' he says, taking a seat next to me. 'All the kids who come to see me do.'

'But I *don't* come to see you . . . Mr Rogers.'

He gives an amused smile. 'I read your story, Robin. *The Tree*.'

'Did you like it?' I say, trying to steer him away from questions about my mother.

'It's very clever,' he replies. 'Black humour. Well written. What's it about?'

'I thought you said you'd read it.'

'I did. What's it about?' he says again.

'Trees.'

He tries once more. 'What's the theme?'

He's playing the literary game. Trying to get under my guard. 'Freedom,' I say.

'The mother tree?'

'Yes, she took off.'

'Why?'

I hesitate. 'Because her family was hopeless. Arguing

and criticising and complaining. They got what they deserved.'

'Maybe there was some other reason she went,' he says slowly.

This comment annoys me. I should know what it's about. I wrote it. 'It's my story,' I say.

'Is it?' he says. 'That's interesting.'

I don't know what he's getting at but I can feel resentment welling up inside me. 'Well, what do *you* think the theme is?' I shoot back.

'It could be about abandonment,' he says.

I spring to my feet. 'I have to go,' I say. 'The bus is here.'

'Robin,' he says, 'I think you have something to tell me. I have no idea what it is but I'd just like you to know that it'll be safe with me if you do.'

'I have nothing to tell you,' I say as I head for the bus. 'But thanks anyway . . . Mr Rogers.'

The next day Dad gives me the day off. I decide to do some downhill skiing. It's still early and the slopes are not too crowded yet. I jostle along in the line with the other earlybirds towards the chairlift.

'G'day, Rick,' I say to the attendant as I get to the front.

He winks at me and gives me the obligatory tap on the shoulder. 'Go, Robin,' he says.

The chair slams into my backside and swings us up into the air. I say 'us' because it's a double chair and there's a girl sitting next to me.

'I didn't arrange this,' says Charlie frostily. 'So don't go getting any ideas.'

I hadn't recognised her in the queue because she's not wearing her red parka but a blue one with the hood up. I'm too amazed to say anything. We both sit in the swaying seat without speaking as it climbs up the mountain above the skiers and snowboarders whooshing silently beneath us. My heart's thumping and my stomach has turned to jelly. Now I've got the chance to explain what happened that day in the forest with the bird – but I have to be careful. Charlie's just as likely to clap her hands over her ears if I say one wrong word.

Or she might even jump off the chair and break a leg or worse.

Think, Robin, think. How are you going to handle this?

Normally a chairlift seems to take ages to get to the top but this ride is rushing by, eating up the time I have to explain. We're already more than halfway up the slope and I still haven't spoken.

Finally I say, 'I thought long and hard before I decided to kill that little bird and . . .' I'm interrupted as our chair bumps more noisily than usual over a pylon. Automatically I glance upwards at the point where it attaches to the cable.

'Liar,' says Charlie. 'You looked upwards. A liar always looks up. Isn't that what your father says?'

The last thing I want to think about is my father. A feeling of hatred towards him grabs me like a vice. Guilt instantly replaces it. I shouldn't hate him. He's my father. You have to love your father, everyone knows that. 'Leave him alone,' I say.

'Okay,' she says. 'Let's talk about you.'

'Me? What have I done?'

'Hanging out with that Verushka.'

'What do *you* care?'

'She's a user. Everyone knows that.'

I don't stop and ask myself if this is true. Instead I continue the attack.

'You don't like anyone except your own group of do-gooders. You're all too holy for people like me and Verushka who don't have both parents waiting hand and foot on them. You and *your* precious dad are perfect.' I shouldn't have said that. Russell's a great guy – I wish *my* old man was like him, but my mouth is running off and I continue to spit out my words. 'You judged me over that bird and yet your own father killed Alf and –'

She cuts me off. 'You heard me apologise to him about Alf. I was wrong. Dad made the hard decision. He loved Alf as much as I did. He didn't want to put him to sleep.'

This is where I should tell her that I tried to put the bird to sleep in the icy water but instead I hear myself snort out a smart-arse reply. 'Put him to sleep. Put him down. Put him to bed. What's the difference?'

'Dad ended Alf's suffering in a gentle and caring way. But what you did was impulsive and cruel and . . .'

The chair starts to rattle. We're reaching the end of the ride. Once again I'm pushing her away.

We lift up the front of our skis so that we can ski off the seat as we reach the platform. In a second we're gliding down the exit ramp, Charlie to the right, me to the left. The cold air is roaring in my ears. She turns away from me. Our roads are parting. I shout at her, giving her back her own words. 'What *you* are doing is impulsive and cruel.'

Her back is disappearing fast. I want to go after her. I was trying to be clever, just using words to win and punish, but I've been cut by her blindness and I'm so angry that I can't contain it. 'Read my bloody letter,' I yell. 'If you've got the guts.'

She speeds away. I'm faster than her on skis and I could catch her if I tried. But I just stand and watch as she becomes airborne off the top of a mogul and vanishes behind it.

I flinch as my lunacy hits me like an icy snowball.

The next morning I decide to cheer myself up with a haircut. I take *The Habit* with me on the bus to do a few revisions as I'm going to enter it into a competition run by the local paper. It's not a bad story and – you never know – I might have a chance.

I go to the unisex place instead of the barber's where I've always gone before. It seems strange at first, sitting in the chair next to a middle-aged woman with foils on her head, but the stylist is pretty cute and she gives me a bit of confidence with her friendly smile. 'How do you want it?' she asks.

'Like that,' I say, pointing to a photograph pinned to the mirror. It's a guy with a cut similar to one in Verushka's book.

'That'll suit you, show off those brown eyes,' she says, giving my scalp a little scratch with the tips of her fingers. That brightens me up. This is another me – a fresh start. My spirits lift even further as my new self evolves in the mirror. When it's finished I stare at the stranger looking back at me.

'Fantastic,' says the stylist. 'Makes you look older.'

She's right. I do look older, and more confident somehow. I give her a grin as I get out my wallet.

Outside birds are singing, kids are laughing, there's not a cloud to be seen. I'm happy to pick up a few groceries in the supermarket for the old man, and even treat myself to a bottle of cheap aftershave.

The bus is only half full for the trip home. I scan the empty seats for a good spot to stretch out. Oh, what! Two unexpected meetings in two days. It's Verushka. She glances up but then looks away.

I'm embarrassed. 'Verushka,' I say. 'How are you going?'

She regards me coolly through those hooded eyes. 'Robin,' she says in a flat voice. 'The jealous writer.'

'Okay if I sit here?' I ask, looking down her low-cut top, even though I shouldn't. I think she's wearing a push-up bra. I try to stop my eyeballs wandering but ever since that night after the art class they seem to have a life of their own.

She shrugs. I shove my pack into the rack above the seats and swing down next to her. 'You were right,' I say first up, to get her on side.

'I usually am.' She stares out of the window but I'm not deterred.

'About the painting,' I say. 'It *was* childish. I'm sorry. I shouldn't have gone on like that.'

Her face totally changes. 'Okay, I forgive you,' she says. 'I like the haircut. You *are* maturing. At last. That jacket's still looking a bit tatty though. You need something to go with those shoes I made you buy.'

We start talking as if nothing happened. I tell her about my meeting with Mr Henderson and how he wants me to see Mr Rogers. Of course I don't mention anything about snapping snakes but she listens carefully to my account. She makes sympathetic murmurings and sort of draws it out of me, all the while patting me on the thigh in a 'there, there' sort of way. She asks me if I've got the story with me.

'Not that one. I've got another one, though.'

'What's it about?'

I think for a moment. 'It's about . . . desire.'

'Let me see it,' she says.

She reads *The Habit* without saying a word. I don't say a word either. It's sort of like 'don't speak until you're spoken to'. I wait for her judgement nervously. I feel as if I've given her a look into my soul.

'It's good,' she says as she turns the last page. 'Your best so far.'

'Really? Do you like it?'

'I just said so, didn't I, dummy? Why do you always doubt yourself? Respect your talent. Go for it. If you don't look out for yourself no one else will.'

'Sorry. Thanks. I'm glad you like it.'

'But you need some advice,' she continues.

'What sort of advice?'

'Do you want to get published?'

'Well, sure, one day maybe. I was going to enter it into that competition run by the *Standard*.'

'Don't bother with that. I can help you get published

and you'll make heaps of money.'

'How?'

'I know someone. He comes to the Polar Bare.'

'Who is he?' I'm suspicious.

'Don't start that again, jealous boy. You're all grown up now, don't forget. He's a literary agent.'

A literary agent. That sounds impressive. 'I can't afford someone like that,' I say, thinking how badly I need this guy and how little I earn from the old man.

'You don't pay up front,' she says. 'He'll take a percentage. And so will I. I do something for you. You do something for me.'

'That sounds fair enough,' I say, thinking what a good day it is and how my luck's changing. Verushka never doubts herself. She's so confident.

She goes on with another bit of advice. 'What you need to do is write creepy stuff and scare the shit out of the reader. It's the black bits in this story that are good but some of it doesn't go far enough. The monk should drown in champagne after ripping the guts out of someone. You need to get into horror. That's where the money is. Look at Stephen King. He's made squillions.'

'I *was* thinking of writing a love story,' I say.

'No, no, no,' she says. 'Do horror. Gordon the Ripper, not Brother Gordon. Love stories are soft.'

'I have to write what comes,' I tell her. 'I can't plan it.'

'Go on, do one for me,' she says putting her hand back on my leg. God, it feels good.

The bus bumps its way slowly up to the snowline and she dozes off. There's no way I'm going to fall asleep with her hand there. I'm too turned on. When the bus reaches the top of the mountain Verushka looks at me with those eyes of hers and flashes a knowing smile. 'One day soon you'll get what you want,' she says.

'I will?'

'Don't look so puzzled, dummy,' she says as she gives my thigh a final squeeze. 'Come over next Saturday night and bring me a horror story.'

I know I have a good imagination. But right now it's in overdrive.

I'm still high when I get home in the afternoon but the old man soon extinguishes my mood. He's drilling out a steel bracket on the workbench.

'Good grief,' he says when he sees me. 'What have you done to your hair? You look like a camel's arse.'

'Don't you ever say anything positive?' I reply. 'It's so depressing working for you. I could just walk off now and go to Melbourne.'

'Go on then. I'm not stopping you.'

'You think I won't?'

'I've seen the way you look at that girl. You're not going to leave here without her.'

'Verushka's leaving at the end of the year. She's been saving up to get a deposit on a rented flat.'

'Not her, the other one who came to tea.'

'Charlie? I was wrong about her.'

'Are you sure about that?'

'Yes, she's nothing to me,' I say as I glance upwards at the ceiling.

'You're a little li . . .' he begins but as he follows my gaze he erupts.

'That bloody swallows' nest. Still there. I've been waiting to see how long it would be before you did what you were told.'

He grabs the icepick from its place on the wall and then drags our stepladder over to the swallows' nest. The legs rock dangerously as he scrambles up and hacks away, furiously sending crumbs of mud and straw flying into the air. I feel like I'm going to explode as my head starts to fill with dreadful images. He takes one last vicious swipe with the icepick. The nest comes free and drops to the floor but the pick continues its swing and unbalances him. The legs of the stepladder suddenly collapse.

'Arrgh,' he yells.

He desperately snatches at the air and manages to grab one of the steel trusses that support the roof. He drops the icepick to the floor and hangs in midair, kicking his legs, trying to find the rungs that aren't there.

'Quick, get the ladder,' he screams out.

The icepick is lying at my feet. His hairy belly is showing between the buttons of his boilersuit. A stinking snake strikes and an image flits across my mind.

It's gone as fast as it came but I'm terrified. Of myself. Of what I might do.

I leave him dangling from the ceiling and run out of the workshop door. The happy skiers and the distant mountains are lost on me as I crouch down outside. I tuck my hands under my armpits to make sure they don't take on a life of their own. I'd momentarily seen myself gutting him with the icepick.

I hear a scraping sound and the clatter of the metal ladder hitting the concrete floor. There's a strangled cry from the workshop and then silence. After a bit I hear a dragging sound followed by my father's limping appearance at the door.

I look at him in horror.

He's staring at me, glasses askew, waving the birds' nest. 'You imbecile. You left me hanging there. What were you trying to do? Kill me?'

If only he knew. I'm not trying to kill him. I'm trying *not* to kill him! I'm petrified that something out of my control will take possession of my arm and make one of my horrific images come to life.

He throws back his own arm to fling the nest in my face. But he stops and then stares into it. He freezes, looks at me aghast and starts to tremble. I wonder what he's seen. It's almost as if he's caught sight of his own twisted face in a mirror and grown ashamed.

The world seems to have stopped turning for us both. One silent tear rolls down his cheek as he opens his arms and beckons me over. What's happening? I climb to my feet and obey, hesitantly. He lets the nest fall to the ground and holds me close. He's never hugged me before. I don't know what to feel but I can't bring myself to hug him back, so I stand there like a sack of wheat, letting him embrace me.

'Sorry, Robin,' he chokes out. 'I'm so sorry.'

He releases me and picks up the nest with trembling hands. He seems at a loss for words.

'It's okay, Dad,' I whisper.

He attempts a smile. 'It's just a nest.'

'Sure, Dad. It's just a nest.'

'We need a holiday,' he says. 'We'll go up north and

get some of that warm, tropical sun. We'll have a great time. You'll see.'

He's being nice to me even though I panicked and left him hanging from the ceiling. I try to sound enthusiastic.

'Great,' I say.

I know we'll never go. Thank goodness.

The incident with the birds' nest shakes me. I ran off and left the old man dangling there. It's not far from actually harming him.

It's hard to know which is worse – having the stinking images or worrying about them after they've gone. The more I think about them the more likely they are to strike. The more often they strike the more likely I am to think about them. I can lie on my bed and imagine a wonderful life – finding my mother, becoming a writer, making love to Verushka. But the delight that these imaginings bring is always ruined by the one thought: Robin, you are insane – something might snap and you'll kill your father or even someone else. Who can say what I'm capable of?

Verushka wants me to write a horror story but I know that writing one will just feed the snakes. For three nights in a row I sit down at the computer but I just can't describe violent deeds. In the end I write a story called *Cereal Killer* which is a comedy about a guy who sells addictive cornflakes.

The visit to Verushka's is the one bright spot on the horizon. I'm spinning out thinking about what might happen there and what didn't happen after she got mad at my reaction to the paintings that night. 'One day soon you'll get what you want.' That's what she said on the bus. Well, I'm not going to get her angry again by showing her the story as soon as I arrive. It's a worry though – Verushka's not one to be put off.

Finally it's Saturday night. Dad is watching the wrestling and already on his second stubby. He knows where I'm going but doesn't raise any protest. 'Have fun,' he says with a hint of sarcasm. Since the episode with the nest he's been preoccupied and vacant and unusually polite to me. Very strange.

I put on my leather jacket and make my way to the youth hostel. Verushka's flat has its own set of outside steps that lead up to a small platform with a door in it. I can hardly bear the suspense as I knock quietly. The door is thrown open. She has on the exotic silk dressing-gown I saw in the art studio. She's excited about something. A thrill runs through me.

'Quick,' she says. 'Come see what I've got for us.'

This is a good start; she hasn't asked to see the story. I drop my pack inside the door and enter the small kitchen-lounge which is lit by flickering candles. There's a door off to one side which I imagine is the bedroom but she leads me over to a couch piled with cushions. We sit down and my heart drops a bit as Verushka tosses a small, tightly sealed plastic bag onto the coffee table. This isn't exactly what I expected.

'What is it?' I say, though I think I know. She looks like a little kid with a bag of lollies.

'Something *very* nice,' she says in her sexy voice.

She opens the package and places what looks like a small piece of horse poop on the table. It's brown and hard like a golf ball. 'Hash,' she exclaims.

'Marijuana?'

'Yes, well, sort of. This is the *real* stuff. The best, really hard to come by and expensive.'

'Where did you get it?' I say, stalling for time but not really wanting to hear the answer.

'Oh, just a guy I know, actually. A new ski instructor, Danny, just back from Amsterdam where this stuff's legal. I had an idea that he might be a smoker. You can tell, but I didn't know him well enough to ask until now. Anyway, he had a few drinks over lunch last week so I asked him and he admitted it. And, I got this off him.'

'How much was it?' is all I can think to say. 'I thought you were saving up your money to get out of here.'

Verushka hesitates for just a second, pulls the silk dressing-gown closed where it's been gradually drifting open and says, 'If you must know, he gave it to me for nothing.' For some reason this makes me anxious.

There's a small tin on the table which she opens to reveal a number of joints. 'I've already rolled them,' she says as she holds one out to me.

I shake my head. 'No thanks, but you go ahead.'

'All the more for me then,' she says happily, lighting up and taking a slow puff. Her eyes become even sleepier than usual.

'What's it like?' I ask.

'Mmm. It's good. Everything is slower and better. Food's better, music is better, jokes are funnier . . . You think wise thoughts, but in the morning you've forgotten what happened. Haven't you ever tried it before? You're such a dummy. Give it a go and see.'

Think wise thoughts? Now I'm interested. Maybe, just maybe, this wisdom could be the cure: wise thoughts driving out horrible pictures.

'What the hell,' I say. 'Why not?'

'Two puffs each and then pass it back,' she says. 'But the person who rolls the joint gets three drags first off – that's the custom.'

She's already had a couple of drags but she takes

another three anyway. 'You know, Robin,' she says dreamily. 'You should write something about me.' She seems to have forgotten all about the horror story she asked me to write. 'Put me in one of your stories.'

'Okay,' I say doubtfully.

'Promise?'

'Promise,' I answer. I think again how beautiful and soft she looks with that gown slipping open.

I puff away tentatively but nothing happens. Verushka laughs when I cough. As we pass the joint between us I relax back into the cushions with her and my mind starts to wander . . . I remember how she gave me that book about how to be cool . . . I thought it was because she cared. But she doesn't really. She couldn't . . . Why did I even think she did? I mean, I don't know anything. I'm dumb next to her . . . She's always telling me what I'm doing wrong. 'Dummy', that's what she calls me . . . My stories aren't right either – just like she says . . . And when she looks at me with those eyes of hers she must be thinking I'm a moron. All I'm good for is to put her in a story. That's all . . . I feel like crap.

It occurs to me that she can read my thoughts . . . This is crazy but I can't stop thinking it . . . I have to stop thinking it . . . but I can't because the idea has taken hold of me . . . Maybe she knows about the unwanted pictures I get in my brain . . .

I'm doomed. I'm a person who can't stop thinking about what I don't want to think about. It can be a bright sunny day and then out of nowhere the clouds appear and it's raining lemon juice . . .

I can sense Verushka's warm body next to mine, but neither of us has anything to say. When is this dope going to kick in? It doesn't work for me . . . Nothing works for me . . . My life is one miserable thing after another . . . I don't have a mother . . . I'm stuck with a pathetic bastard of a father who just wants to control me and who carried on about a stupid nest that I forgot to knock off the wall . . . And Charlie wants nothing to do with me even though I sold my mother's ring to give her the money . . . It's no wonder I feel like shit most of the time . . . We're on the third joint and I'm not feeling wise and that everything's better like Verushka said. You can't believe anything she says . . . She just gets off on playing around with me . . . Why am I even here? She doesn't want to look at my story . . . She's no better than my father.

I suddenly get a flash of me sticking the burning end of the joint into my own eye. I make to get up but the cushions are too soft.

'How is it?' says Verushka sleepily. 'Good stuff, huh?'

'Nothing's happening,' I tell her. 'It's not doing anything.'

'You have to take it right down,' she says. 'Don't just puff. Don't you know anything?'

I draw twice right down into my lungs but it's no good . . . Everything's the same as usual, my mind's in turmoil with it all . . . I know now that if I don't leave this mountain I'll kill my father. I won't be able to stop myself . . . Something'll click in my brain and my hand and the icepick will do the rest.

My stomach's heaving and I lean over the coffee table.

'Now what?' says Verushka.

'You don't *really* like me,' I say. 'You're just messing with me.'

She laughs. 'You're getting paranoid,' she says. 'Dope can do that.'

'I feel sick,' I moan.

Verushka jumps up. 'Oh no. You're greening out. Quick, take deep breaths. Really deep.'

I've never felt so sick in my life. I breathe in and out, gulping down the air like a drowning man.

Gradually my stomach settles down and I lie back on the cushions again and change the topic. 'That's a really lovely dressing-gown,' I say. 'But it's a bit big for you.'

'It's Ryan's,' Verushka tells me in her matter-of-fact way. 'You should get one like it. They're cool. I love a sophisticated man who wears one after a shower or after . . .' She doesn't finish the sentence but sits there in the candlelight lost in her own thoughts.

Who does she think I am? As if I'd ever wear anything like that. If she wants me to be another Ryan then I'm out of here. 'I don't think I'll have any more dope,'

I say as I push myself up off the sofa. 'I don't think it's my thing.'

'I made them too strong,' she says. 'I forgot that you're still just a kid who works for his father.'

The word *father* makes me tremble. The horrible images of the icepick flicker in my mind like the light from Verushka's candles. It's never been this bad before.

'I'm giving it a miss,' I say as I fumble my way to the door. 'But you smoke it whenever you want,' I add, snatching up the bag containing my manuscript.

'Thanks very much,' she says from her bed of cushions. 'How generous of you.'

I go out and throw up in the snow.

When I get back home I'm still a little nauseous and have a bit of a headache but it's not too bad. Gradually I settle down enough to think about writing. I sit at the computer to write a story about Verushka like she wanted. I'm not going to follow any prescriptions. I'm the writer and I do whatever comes into my head.

I'm going to write something true. The way *I* see it. Yes, I know what I'll do. I give a chuckle and start to tap away on the keyboard.

I change names and places so that no one else will know it's her – that's only fair. It takes me nearly all night to write the story and by the time I finish the lights are going out on the freshly groomed ski slopes.

The ice on the window reminds me of the image I saw there of Mum. I jump up and take her hairbrush out of the hiding place under the bottom drawer. Then I just lie in bed, holding it and letting the thought of her wash away all the negative feelings about Verushka.

After a bit I put the brush on the bed and get dressed. I print off my manuscript and head outside into the cold air. My footprints are the only ones in the virgin snow as I make my way back to Verushka's flat and slip the story she asked for under her door. As I return home I see that a few early rays of sunshine are stealing the darkness from the long cold night.

# The Jacket

Mate, I tell ya. I loved me old bomber jacket. Okay, it was from way back when and the leather was worn on the elbows like a monkey's bum. But you could tell that it had had a life. A hard life but a good life. You know – patina – cracks and lines on it like a warrior's face.

Sometimes I would imagine the blokes who had it before me. Maybe one was a stunt pilot. Or maybe the leader of a bikie gang or a general like Montgomery or Monash from years back in the Second World War. It had history written all over it – definitely a real man's jacket. They sell new ones like it in posh Collins Street shops but the wear is artificial and you can tell it's not the real thing. You can't buy experience. Ya have to earn it, if ya know what I mean.

If anyone tried to nick that jacket, mate, I'd have gone through them like a dose of salts. Me and that jacket were brothers. Never to be separated.

Where one goes the other goes.

It suited me image too. Just the shot for a muso. What with me working man's boots, me black T-shirt, me brass diving watch and the cool sunnies, I was the lad to be like. Okay, a bit wild looking with long hair and a beard. I was a bit on the hairy side. But hey – I was in a rock band. When I sat behind those drums I was somethin' else, I can tell ya.

Well, that's what I reckoned at the time. Bein' young an' cocky I thought I knew it all. But the truth was that me and the lads had only played at one gig and that was at a mate's party and we didn't get paid a cent for it. But we had hopes. Hopes but no money. But ya can't eat hopes, can ya?

Look, I'll come clean at the start. In the end we did make it big. Not as big as AC/DC or Paul Kelly. But nearly. Money, travel, fame. The lot. But in the early days it wasn't like that. No way. You never know whether yer going to make it big or not.

Anyways, I was on the dole. I lived over a fish-and-chip shop for nuthin' except that I had to do the dishes every night. Me girlfriend's name was Emily and she used to stay overnight with me off and on.

Gees, I had the hots for her. She was a real babe but no wimp, if ya know what I mean. Like she was strong minded. Right from the start she told me, 'I've got a friend called Michael. He works in a bank. Now don't go getting jealous. He's just a friend. We have lunch together every week. There's nothing more to it than that. Nothing physical.'

Well, I have to say that I did get a bit jealous. I only met the guy twice. He was just the opposite to me, ya know. Like, he wore this pin-striped suit and a coloured business shirt and tie. He had shiny, pointy shoes and wore a gold watch. And he went to the hairdresser's every week – I mean really. And he sported one of those slick haircuts and was shaved real close, like. Smooth as a baby's backside he was. Not a hairy bloke at all. Me, I was covered in the stuff.

Also, and at the time it was a worry, I can say that now, Michael had a few bob to spare. He traded shares and stuff and could take Emily out for a slap-up meal. Gees, all I was good for was a pie and sauce after the footy. She liked this guy, Michael, I could tell. She lent me this book of his all about nerds and what they wore and what the cool 'metrosexuals' wore. It was supposed to be funny but it sucked, to be honest.

One morning when we were in bed all soft and warm and that, Emily says, 'Hey Gordon, you've got hair in your ears.'

'Oh yeah,' I say.

'You should pull them out.'

'It's a bit hard to see,' I say.

'I'll do it,' she says.

So she gets a pair of tweezers and pulls out the hairs in my ears. One at a time. It hurt a bit but not much – I mean I'm no wimp either. Once I said 'ouch' and she laughed. She had a lovely laugh. God, I loved it.

Not long after that she says, 'I'm going to buy you a watch for your birthday. That old diving watch is real cheap and it has the brass showing through.'

'Wow,' I said. 'That's real nice of you.' She was kind that way, she was.

'What sort would you like?' she says.

'Well, an explorer's watch with three or four small dials showing the altitude and the diving depth and which way's north. It can tell the time too, if you want,' I added for a joke. 'But don't get gold. I don't go for gold on men.'

Soon after that Emily goes, 'Why don't you get some pointy shoes? Italian. All the guys are wearing them. Those boots aren't cool these days.'

'Give me a break,' I say. 'I'm in a rock band.'

'Just for special occasions,' she goes. 'When you take me out.'

Well, I can tell you they weren't cheap, those shoes. And they weren't comfy. But I bought them because I didn't want her going off me, like. I mean, if she dropped me and started going with that Michael guy, I would have died.

Not too long after this we're at the beach. 'You know, Gordon,' she says, 'your shoulders are a bit hairy. You should get them waxed.'

'Waxed?'

'Yes, you'll be nice and smooth,' she says. 'I admire that in a man. Michael is smooth.'

So there I am as embarrassed as hell lying on a bench in a beauty salon. This sheila all dressed in white is tearing at my shoulders with a strip of cloth covered in some sort of hot goo. Gawd, this time it did hurt. Not that I'm a wimp, mind you.

But anyways, not to worry. It was my birthday and when I got home Emily presents me with my lovely watch. It was flat and thin with a single dial and a case made of gold. Must have cost a packet. She was generous that way was Emily.

Well, by now you are getting the picture. It's not long before I have a slick haircut. And a business shirt and tie.

'You look great,' says Emily. 'Michael is younger than you but you're much more handsome than him with that new haircut.'

It's funny but every time she mentioned his name I got jealous. I couldn't help it. But I didn't say anything because she would crack the sads.

All this happened over about six months. I was gradually changing into someone else. Maybe I was turning into a guy who works in an office. But I didn't care that much. I was crazy about Emily. It was worth it to look how she wanted me to. And I mean, that guy, Michael – he was always in the back of my mind. Emily kept on telling me how great he was. Even if nothing 'physical' *was* happening.

Finally I'm getting around to the big one. You guys must have seen it coming.

'I've been invited to a wedding,' says Emily. 'One of my friends. I want you to take me.'

'No worries,' I say.

'But you'll have to get a suit,' says Emily. 'Otherwise I'll ask Michael to take me. You understand, don't you? You couldn't go to a Toorak wedding in that old bomber jacket. I'd be so embarrassed.'

I hung my head. 'I could *hire* a suit, I suppose,' I said.

Emily shook her head. Gawd, she had lovely hair. '*Buy* one,' she said. 'Then you can wear it when we go out. All the guys have got pin-striped suits. It's the look.'

Oh man, I suffered. Oh shit, I agonised. It was awful. I didn't want to let her down but I couldn't afford a suit. On the other hand I couldn't stand the thought of that wimp Michael taking her to the wedding. I couldn't borrow that much dough either. And I didn't have a thing I could sell. Well, that ain't quite true. In the end I went to a second-hand shop. I couldn't believe the words that was coming out of my cakehole.

'How much will ya give me for the jacket?'

'Well, look,' goes the guy in the shop. 'It's well worn. And old. But these bomber jackets are sought after these days. I could go a hundred bucks.'

So that's how me and my old bomber jacket were parted. I bought meself a pin-striped suit to go with my smooth shoulders and slick haircut and the pointy shoes and the gold watch and the business shirt and tie. But it was worth it for Emily. Wasn't it?

I looked at myself in the mirror. Ya couldn't pick me from a real business executive.

I made up me mind to go and wait for Emily outside her work. To surprise her with my new suit and stuff. On the way I met Possum. He plays lead guitar in our band.

His eyes nearly popped out when he saw me in my new gear. Then he looked sad. 'Listen man,' he said. 'The guys have asked me to talk to you. It's about the band. You're losing your touch. You're not playing wild any more. We was wondering whether you still wanted to play with us. Like . . . well, you know . . .'

His voice trailed off. I caught sight of meself in the window of a bank. Some other guy stared back at me – Bank Man. I felt as if I'd got stones in my pockets and was sinking to the bottom of a deep well.

I gave Possum a rough shove. 'Come and have a drink, mate,' I said.

We walked over the road to The Pig and Whistle and I ordered two beers. Right at that moment I caught sight of someone I thought I recognised. A wild-looking guy in jeans and boots with scruffy hair. For a sec I thought it was me. He was wearing an old diving watch and . . . and . . . wait for it . . . my bomber jacket!

I couldn't believe it. Who *was* this guy? I knew I'd seen him before.

'Michael!' I yelled.

'Gordon!' he screamed.

'What are ya dressed up like that for?' I asked.

'Trying to keep up with you, old son. Emily wanted to go to a rock concert. Told me that if I wouldn't look the part, she'd get *you* to take her. I was as jealous as hell. Even though she told me you were just a friend. Nothing . . .'

'Physical?' I said.

He nodded.

Knowingly.

We just stood there looking at each other for a few seconds. Guys in the pub started to gather around. They could sense a fight.

'Same for me,' I said. 'Only it was a wedding.'

'You look like an idiot in that suit, old chap,' he said.

'And you're a total dork in that bomber jacket, mate. Where did ya get it?'

'Emily found it in a second-hand shop. I was planning to buy a new one but she came up with this.'

'It's mine,' I said.

We stared at each other like two boxers squaring up. But each of us was thinking. Big thoughts.

Suddenly he bent down and pulled off his boots. He threw them at me. One hit me in the chest. 'You can have these, old sport,' he yelled.

I ripped off the pointy Italian shoes. 'And you can have these, mate.' I threw them at him. He caught both of 'em easily.

I started to pull down the pin-striped pants. Everyone in the bar gaped. They thought it was hilarious. I dropped me pants and threw them at his feet. He grinned and had the jeans off in half a second. The whole pub roared as we began to strip.

'You can have the pin-striped pants,' I yelled.

'And you can have the jeans.'

'You can have the bloody gold watch.'

'And you can have the ratty old diving monstrosity.'

'You can have the coloured shirt and tie.'

'And you can have the black T-shirt.'

Then came the big one.

'You can have the pin-striped suit coat.'

There was no pause at all.

'And you can have this worn-out bomber jacket.'

In no time at all we were dressed as we should be.

He was himself. And so was I.

There was only one thing more. We both yelled exactly the same words at each other at exactly the same time.

'And you can have Emily!'

Oh, how we laughed.

You should have been there. It was so good, mate. So good.

I just can't tell ya.

# THE NEST

## 5

Dad's already in the workshop when I return from putting the story under Verushka's door. He has a lot of work due out today and he's getting an early start. I suddenly remember I didn't put Mum's hairbrush away before I went out. Oh, hell, what if he went in my room? It's the sort of thing he does. Snooping. I race upstairs to look for it. It's gone. I rush down and find Dad sitting at his desk in the workshop.

'Where's Mum's hairbrush?' I shout at him.

He turns around on his swivel chair and looks at me with steely eyes. He reaches into a drawer, takes out the brush and hands it to me. I snatch it back and though I have it safe and sound something's changed – the strands of Mum's hair have gone. What's wrong with him? Why on earth did he take the brush and clean it and then give it straight back?

'Do you hate her so much that you have to get rid of every trace?' I yell.

'Don't ever speak to me like that,' he says in a low, menacing voice.

I'm left feeling foolish. I almost apologise for shouting at him but some instinct tells me that I've been wronged and that it's he who owes *me* an apology. And an explanation. I'm sick of him shutting down every time I mention my mother. I'm entitled to know. She *is* my mother.

I take a breath and try to sound normal. 'Why doesn't Mum ever send me a birthday present or even a card? She could be dead for all I know.'

'Not this again,' he moans. 'I've told you a hundred times: don't ask about the past. What's gone is gone.'

'I want to find her. Dad, I know it hurts you but I have a right. I'm old enough to handle the truth.'

'If she cared about you she'd have contacted you by now. Don't go on about it.'

'Where did she go? She must have told you where she is now.'

'How would I know? I looked everywhere for the bitch. She's with another man probably. She was a . . . flirt.'

Bitch. Flirt. I'm stung by his words and I let him see it.

'She went because you're a cold-hearted bastard.'

His voice is controlled and his words deliberate. ' I told you. It wasn't *me* she left, Robin. It was *you*. Crying and screaming every night. It got her down. She was always tired and miserable. She couldn't hack it. She wanted the good life. She was in the Polar Bare Club all the time. She didn't want a child.

'It wasn't me,' I shout. 'She loved me.'

I know that *he* knows he's gone too far.

'Don't go on about her, Robin. It just brings it all

back. She really hurt me. She left me. She left you. Some people are just hopeless and she's one of them. If she came back you wouldn't like her. If you really care about me you'll never mention her name again.'

I feel as if I'm tumbling down a dark, deep hole.

'I think you drove her away,' I say more quietly now. 'You told her to go.'

I'm expecting rage. I'm expecting shouting. Maybe he'll hit me. He never has but who knows what he could do if he snapped? I must get my own violence from somewhere. Finally he says, 'Okay, you asked for it.'

He walks back to the little nook where he hid the hairbrush, pulls a bunch of keys out of his pocket and slides up the lid of his rolltop desk. Inside are papers and cheque books and a carved wooden box. He unlocks the box, takes out a faded envelope and extracts a letter. It's a single page, folded once. He hands it to me and I stare at the elegant handwriting.

All this time he's had a letter from her and he's kept it from me! These words on the paper are her words. Her fingers held the pen that traced out every letter.

Her hand made the fold. I tremble as I read the short message from the past:

*Alan,*

*It's all too much. I'm leaving you. Don't try to find us because I have taken steps to make sure you can't. I'll contact you when we're settled. You will be much happier without me. There is nothing more to say except goodbye.*

*Miranda*

'See,' I cry. 'She says it's all too much. You're her husband. You're the guilty one.' I'm trembling because this is something concrete, something to latch on to. And because it makes mention of me.

'It says "us. Don't try to find us". She wouldn't leave me with you. She took me with her.'

'You've got it all wrong,' he says. 'Listen to what I'm saying. I've been trying to protect you. She went off with another man, Robin. She left us for one of her boyfriends. I didn't want to tell you. But you just had to know the truth. And now you do. I came home one day to find that note. All her things were gone.'

Another man? I don't believe him. He's a liar. I don't trust him at all. She wouldn't leave me for a lover.

'It says "I will contact you",' I tell him.

'Well, she hasn't, has she? That says it all. She doesn't give a sparrow's fart about either of us.'

'I'm going to find her and then we'll see.' My voice is rising again. So is his.

'Just stop for a minute, Robin. Think. Who feeds you? Who's here for you? Who pays the bills? Who's slaving away night and day? What about me? What about giving something back to me? What's *she* ever done for you? She's a tramp. She abandoned you.'

'You're lying,' I yell. I pick up a screwdriver and wave it at him.

His face turns white and little veins stand out on his nose. For a second I think he might burst a blood vessel. Or I will. He draws a breath as if he's about to rush into battle but then he pauses. 'What are you going to do with that? Stab me?' He gives a scornful laugh.

The world is spinning. My hands are trembling. I throw the screwdriver to the ground as if it's a live snake and charge out into the fresh, clean air of a beautiful mountain morning.

And bump straight into Verushka. She's holding my manuscript. She takes three or four pages of my story, rips them in half and then throws them into the air. The torn pages fall to the ground like dead butterflies. She throws down the remaining pages and stamps them into the snow.

'You creep,' she screams. She turns and sweeps off across the slope.

After the exchange with my father, her rage seems nothing at all. It's strange really. I start to laugh. I laugh and laugh until my stomach hurts. I'm hysterical. The story did the trick for me – it put Verushka into perspective. Writing is the only thing that seems to save me from going crazy.

I rush back up to my room, turn on the computer

and begin to write. I don't know what the story will be about but something will come. My fingers start tapping and the words *The Birds* appear on the screen.

Over the next two weeks, Dad seems even more distant than usual. In fact he's acting really weird. He's been closing the workshop every day. When I get home from school it's always locked up. He comes home late on the Ski-Doo and he's evasive about where he's been.

But what's he up to? I'm intrigued. I learn a little more the next time I walk across the slope to fetch the mail. The post office consists of one tiny window at the back of the ski-hire business, which is quite handy because it's open on weekends. Lovely old Mary and Don Baker handle all the mail on the mountain, and it's Mary who lets me into a bit of the mystery.

'Is your dad off birdwatching again?' she asks.

'What?' I say. 'He's not the slightest bit interested in

birds. He wouldn't care if every single one disappeared from the face of the earth.'

'Well, according to Don, he's been up near the mine looking for swallows.'

'Really? In the snow?'

'That's what he said when they bumped into each other in the forest. They had a discussion about birds and the best sort of binoculars for spotting them.'

I'm at a loss. I don't like the sound of it. I try to laugh it off. 'He must be turning into a greenie,' I say.

'Like you,' she laughs. 'And your friend Charlie.'

Mrs Baker's always calling me a greenie because I once signed a petition to keep snowmobiles out of the state forest even though my part-time job is helping Dad repair them. My stomach contracts at the sound of Charlie's name. She's a *real* greenie.

Mrs Baker hands me a bundle of letters. 'None for you, Robin. Mostly bills by the look of it. Hey, are you okay? You look worried.'

I shove the letters into my pocket. 'I'm fine, Mrs B. Just trying to imagine my dad birdwatching, that's all.'

Back home in my room I put the last touches to my story. It just needs a little editing, so I'm soon finished with it. When I get a spare moment I'll take it to some quiet place in the bush and read over it. I slip the printed manuscript into a plastic sleeve, fold it and put it in my parka pocket. The letters from the post office are still there. I take them out and shuffle through them. They're all windowpane envelopes except for one sealed letter. It's addressed to my father. I turn it over and read the name of the sender: George and Sanderson Pathology Laboratory, 22/530 Spring Street, Mowbray.

Goosebumps form on my arms as I take in the word 'pathology'. Is my dad ill? Is that why he gave me that hug? What if he has cancer or some other dreadful disease? Is that why he's off on the Ski-Doo, living it up on his last few days?

Outside, I hear the workshop door open and slam closed again. He's returned. I take the stairs two at a time and hurry to the workshop with the letters.

'You packed up early,' he says accusingly. 'As soon as I'm out of sight . . .'

'Mail,' I say, interrupting him and shoving the letters towards him.

He takes the mail to his desk to read and I trail behind. 'What's that one?' I say as he opens the letter from the pathology laboratory.

He turns ashen as he reads it.

'It's personal,' he grunts.

'Are you sick?'

'No.'

He puts the letter in the wooden box where he keeps his documents and locks it in the rolltop desk.

'What is it then?'

'Don't you ever take no for an answer?' he says, closing the conversation for good.

That night I turn over the possibilities. What if he's dying? He's not much of a father but I don't want him to die. I know what the word pathology means but I grab my worn copy of the Macquarie Dictionary and check anyway. It has three definitions: **Pathology.** n. **1.** the science of the origin, nature, and course of diseases. **2.** the conditions and processes of a disease.

**3.** the study of morbid or abnormal mental or moral conditions.

My whole body freezes as I read number three. It's not my father who's sick – it's me. I knew it. I've got an abnormal mental and moral condition. Dad knows. He knows I'm an insane person who gets murderous images flashing into his head. I take this knowledge to bed with me – all night my mind churns it over and over and refuses to allow me sleep.

I feel no better in the morning when I realise that my father will refer me to some specialist, a doctor or psychiatrist who'll diagnose insanity. Dad'll probably be glad to get rid of me. He seems more interested in birds anyway. I bet he goes off again today.

I'm not wrong. Straight after breakfast he says, 'You're in charge.' He heads towards the yellow Ski-Doo which is spluttering impatiently outside the workshop door.

'Where are you going?' I ask, not sure if I can handle being on my own. Or maybe it's safer if I *am* on my own.

'Out,' he says as he mounts the machine. It leaps forward and he disappears up the slope.

I turn back into the workshop and see that the sharpened icepick isn't hanging in its place. Just like that, an image bites my brain – the icepick in my hand, sinking into Dad's head. I moan. What's wrong with me? Something bad's going to happen. I can't bear it anymore. I need to know what's going on.

I grab a pinch bar and walk over to the desk where he keeps his mail and shove the end of it under the rolltop. There's the sound of splintering and the lid springs up ripping white wounds into the brown wood. The carved wooden box is inside. I snatch it and put it on the floor, then lift the pinch bar in the air and smash it open, letting loose another snake bite inside my head. It flashes away as I see the letter lying next to the open box. I scan the pages. The letter isn't signed. The last page is missing.

I skim over the formal stuff which consists of a whole lot of graphs and statistics. I read something about sample MG 1A and MG 2B. They seem to be a match.

What does this mean? I think I know. My father's sent off a sample of my DNA – a fingernail clipping or a hair or saliva on a tissue – and they've tested it. I ought to know more about DNA testing, but I don't. I'm probably missing a chromosome or something. The same chromosome that's missing from other weirdos and maniacs who see horrific images.

It's confirmed. I *am* mad.

Negative thoughts overwhelm me. I try to distract myself by thinking about my mother. I try to imagine her face and her smile but it's no good. Why did she abandon me? Why? Why? Why? I have to get my mind off the misery that possesses me.

I'm going to follow him, confront him if I have to. I lock up the workshop, take down my skis and put on my parka and beanie. I have to hurry. There's no time for emergency gear; I'm in too much of a frenzy anyway.

The brightest of cold blue skies lies behind and above the white peaks of the snowfields. One or two clouds threaten but they're far off and anyway I'm beyond caring. I put on my cross-country skis and head uphill passing under the chairlift with its load of carefree skiers. An engineer is repairing a window in the shelter by the lower ramp. He's rugged up against the freezing air in a thick snow suit and gloves. He fumbles with a tape measure and drops it in the snow. He seems to glower at me as he bends to pick it up. A lightning image hits me and I see myself plunge a knife straight into his chest. Where did this come from? The poor man's totally innocent.

'I will not kill Dad,' I say to myself. 'They're just thoughts. They're not real.'

Please let this be true.

A signpost with five fingers identifies various ski trails. Some of them lead up to the peaks and others down into the valley. It makes me think of a giant white hand showing the way to heaven. Or hell. I wince as another violent image flashes.

One of the signs reads: *Finnegan's Forest Walk 10 km*. This is my route. The one that leads uphill along the bush trail to Old Baldy, then plummets down through thick stands of snow gums and past the lake before ending at Logan's Refuge which is close to the mine.

As I turn onto the track I see a lone figure in a red

parka watching my progress. The skier beckons to me. For a second I think it might be Charlie but she wouldn't wave at me. I peer but can't see who it is – maybe someone trying to indicate that I shouldn't be setting out without a pack. I have no time for anyone. My mind's in a black fog. The trees seem to have faces.

The narrow walking track is covered in about twenty centimetres of snow – nothing I can't handle in this weather. The first signs of spring are making themselves known. Unseen streams gurgle beneath the surface and every now and then a bent branch releases its load with a heavy swoosh.

Soon I'm hot and my parka and beanie become burdens. Rivers of sweat run inside my T-shirt and boxers. I can't stop thinking about the violent images that come from somewhere deep inside me. Will I act one out? How can I stop them? I know that struggling against them gives them strength so in the end I just let them buzz in and out of awareness. There's nothing I can do. My fate is already written. It's built into my DNA.

An hour passes and no sign of my father. My legs

ache from the effort of sliding one ski in front of the other on the unforgiving slopes. I pass White Mountain Cemetery where the fifty or so tombstones in a clearing wear thin hats of snow that sparkle in the sunshine. Most of the headstones lean like frozen drunks. They're green with moss and many have inscriptions worn away by the fierce mountain storms.

Now I've broken out of the trees and I'm heading up over the bare slopes of Old Baldy. For an instant I have an image of my father's bare head but it's driven away by the sight of black clouds racing towards the peak. I must hurry. I reach the summit after half an hour more and bend my shoulders into the wind which has sprung up. It begins to snow heavily. I zip my parka collar up over my mouth and pick up speed as I head downhill into Finnegan's Forest trail. I wonder what I will find when I reach the old mineshaft.

Once again I'm surrounded by trees and am a little protected from the wind. I reach the shore of the lake. Thin, patchy ice covers the surface. Black streaks of water appear here and there like holes in a moth-eaten jumper. A bent tree is a solitary angler standing on a white shore. I drop onto the snow for a moment or two and realise how tired I am. I feel weak and my head is spinning. I'm not even sure what I'm doing here or what I expect to find.

Weird thoughts flit through my mind like frightened birds bursting from their hideouts. The snow is heavy and cold and wet on my face. I begin to shiver as I push on and soon leave the lake behind.

The sky overhead is dark and threatening. The wind has dropped and gentle snowflakes flurry about my head. I know that I shouldn't be up here without a tent and a shovel and an icepick, but the turn-off to the mine where I hope to find my father isn't far now. Without warning sleet and hail begin to lash my face. The last patches of warmth drain from my body. I have to get out of this or I will die. Stupid, stupid, stupid, coming up here without a backpack and supplies.

My goggles are now so covered in snow and ice that I can hardly see anything more than a dim whiteness but when I take them off the frozen sleet drives into my eyes and I still can't see. I squint and vaguely make out a rectangular shape ahead of me. The refuge. Saved! I push myself against the ripping wind and reach the door. With a slight feeling of guilt I break the glass emergency lock so I can get in. I don't know why I'm feeling guilty. An emergency like this is just what the hut's here for.

I pull off my skis, stagger inside and look around in the gloom. There are no windows along the white-washed walls and the snowstorm outside throws little light through the flapping door. In the centre of the room I can just make out a strong wooden table with a kerosene lamp standing in the centre. Next to it is a flame gun used for lighting gas ovens. I memorise the layout with one quick glance and then fight to close the open door which has let the blizzard follow me into the room. Now I'm in total darkness. I grope around and grab the flame gun. I press the trigger and a lazy flame throws enough light for me to fire up the kerosene lamp. I see a fireplace set with kindling and wood and matches. There are rough cupboards and six bunks with blankets and sleeping-bags and towels neatly folded on the end of each. There's even an old stuffed leather sofa in front of the fireplace. I open a cupboard and see tins of soup and stews and other food. There are enough provisions here for a handful of people to ride out the longest storm.

My feelings of panic begin to subside now that I'm safe. I hear the anger of the storm through the log walls and remember that Dad's out there somewhere. I hope he's found shelter. He has the icepick and he knows what he's doing. When there's a break in the storm he'll head here for sure. I'll give him until my clothes dry out – then I'll have to go and look for him, no matter how bad the weather gets.

I squat down in front of the fireplace and click the flame gun which throws its tongue at the crumpled paper under the kindling. Nothing happens. Shit. The paper's damp. I'm not worried because I know I can get it going but I'm cold and I want that fire started. Fast. I whirl around looking for paper and then remember that my manuscript's inside my parka pocket. I pull out the plastic sleeve and crumple up the A4 sheets.

It's only eight pages but that's enough to do the trick and flames are soon licking the kindling and drying the damp newspaper above it.

I feel apprehensive as I watch my story turn to smoke and curl up the chimney. I can always print out another copy so that's not what's gnawing at me. Maybe it's the thought of the icepick but I don't think so. It's something to do with my mother and father. The flames seem to form dancing pictures of their faces yelling at each other. The fire is illustrating the very tale that it's consuming. I get this crazy idea that the story about the birds holds the answer to the mystery of my mother's whereabouts. This is mad because *I* wrote the story and made up everything that's in it. It all came out of my own head so how can it hold the answer?

I remember my discussion with Mr Rogers about *The Tree*. I said, 'It's *my* story,' meaning that *I* wrote it. He replied, 'That's interesting.' His words had a double meaning – he was implying the story about the trees was autobiographical. But that can't be right. *The Birds* came from nowhere. It doesn't mean anything. I retrace the story about the birds in my mind, searching for a clue, but nothing occurs to me.

I think back to the conversation at Charlie's house and remember how Russell said that animals do things without thinking. A dingo might go down to the waterhole where small animals drink in the evening. The dingo doesn't say to itself, 'The wallabies will be here tonight.' The dingo knows without knowing that it knows. Can a *person* know something without knowing it?

The heat from the fire begins to take possession of the room. I take off my wet parka and dry myself with a towel. I pull on some warm clothes from the emergency supply and hang my wet gear in front of the fire. I'm hardly aware of the howling wind outside. I lie down on the old leather sofa. Exhaustion claims me and I'm soon asleep.

# The Birds

Up in Queensland there was a young boy named Gordon who was mad about birds. He used to go watching them with binoculars in the forest. He had books about them. He took photographs. He drew birds – even in those days he had an interest in painting. He was a fanatic about saving their habitats.

Anyway, one day he learned about a pair of rare Restless Finches that were kept in a small cage by a shady character called Ratnally who lived on Mud Island in the middle of the estuary.

'He's a smuggler,' says the boy. 'He'll put them in a sock or a small box and smuggle them overseas. Restless Finches are worth thousands. We have to save them.'

'Don't you go getting any ideas,' says his mother.

'It's against the law,' says the boy. 'Those birds are protected. And it's cruel. Most of them die before they reach their destination.'

'You can't prove a thing,' says the boy's mother. 'It's his island. Don't you set foot there.'

'They'll be laying soon,' says the boy. 'The eggs won't hatch in a small cage without a nest.'

'Just don't even think about letting them out,' says his mother.

'I can't,' says the boy. 'Restless Finches aren't from around here. They live in the mountains. They'll die if you let them out in the wrong habitat.'

'It's not our problem,' says his mother. 'Just mind your own business.'

The boy doesn't say anything because his mother is already mad at him for getting a weird haircut. She doesn't like it so modern.

So he figures that what she doesn't know won't hurt her. He decides that he will rescue the birds and take them back into the mountains where they come from. The only problem is, he doesn't have a boat to get to the island.

But what he does have is an old bath that's out in the backyard. It was once used as a horse trough. He gets the bath and glues a plug into the drain hole. Then he finds a small metal coffee table in their shed and plonks it in the bath.

'In case it rains,' he says to himself.

The boy also grabs a large plastic packet of birdseed and a bottle of water.

That night, around midnight, he sneaks down to the mangrove swamp, pulling the bath behind him on a little trailer.

It is wild and desolate country. Feral pigs, crocodiles, massive goannas – you name it. He has to be careful.

But it's only a short distance to the island so thinks he will be okay. He uses two table-tennis bats to paddle the bath over the river at high tide when there's no current running. When he gets to the island he drags the bath up the muddy beach to stop it floating away.

At that moment the moon comes out. Most of the island is wooded but he knows there is a clearing around the house which he'll have to sneak across. If he gets seen it could be serious. Ratnally is a thug. And he has a shotgun.

The boy has seen a lot of movies so he knows what to do. He takes off all his clothes and covers himself with black mud. Now he's camouflaged like a jungle fighter. But he is totally naked. He even takes off his shoes so that they don't make a noise if he steps on a twig or something.

Anyway, he sneaks up to Ratnally's bungalow like a black

ghost in a coalmine. There are the two finches in a small cage just inside the window. The night is silent. The boy quietly takes off the fly-wire screen and gently lifts out the cage.

The birds begin to squawk.

'Shhh . . .' says the boy.

But it's too late. A light goes on in a nearby room. The boy runs for it, belting across the clearing as fast as he can go.

'Come back, you bastard,' roars Ratnally. There's a blast from a shotgun. Pellets fly overhead. One hits the poor boy in the bum.

*Blam.* Another blast. By this time the boy is into the trees and the pellets smash harmlessly into the bush off to one side.

The boy's feet are bleeding and the cage is banging against his naked thigh and the finches are squawking like crazy. He belts down to the mudflats, puts the cage into the bath and pushes out into the stream leaving his clothes behind him on the muddy shore.

By this time the tide is running out. The boy paddles like a madman with his table-tennis bats but the rushing water's too strong. In no time at all, the bath is heading out to sea. There's no way the boy can fight against the current. It is hopeless.

In the end he gives up paddling and falls back against the steel table, exhausted. He watches as the stars slowly circle in the sky above. Eventually he falls asleep.

When he awakes he sits up and looks around.

The sky above is blue. The ocean all around is blue. There is no sign of land. How long he's been asleep he doesn't know. Which way it is to the land he has no idea. The finches regard him silently.

There is not a breath of wind. The sea is totally flat. The bath rocks gently whenever he moves. He knows that if the wind gets up there will be waves. And if they are rough the bath will sink. He will die and the birds will die with him.

But on this score, for the time being, he need not worry. The sea is as flat as a concrete floor. He is becalmed.

He tips some water into the birds' drinking container and gives them a little bit of seed. They look at him with beady eyes.

'Don't worry,' he says. 'I'll get you home.'

But about this he is not so sure. He can't let the birds out of the cage because if they fly off they might not reach the shore. And even if they do, it is a long way to the mountains where they come from.

A day passes. And then another. Still the sea is flat. Now his water is running out. By this time he is really worried.

But that night the rain starts to fall from the heavens. By morning the water in the bath is up to his ankles. He fills up the bottle and tops up the birds' water. His head is bent low, just touching the edge of the cage. Suddenly he feels a little pain on the top of his head. And then another.

The finches. It's the finches. They each hold a little tuft of his hair in their beak.

For a second or two he can't take it in.

'Oh, no,' he says. 'You're nesting.'

He looks around the bath. There's nothing. Absolutely nothing for them to make a nest out of. He knows at once that if eggs are laid on the tin floor of the bath they won't hatch. The metal won't retain enough heat. He looks at the plastic bag containing the birdseed. He could tear that up but there'd be nowhere to put the seed and it'd get wet in the bath. If he tips the seed onto the table and the wind gets up it could blow away. And anyway, a plastic bag wouldn't provide enough insulation to incubate the eggs.

The poor boy doesn't know what to do. He can't bear the thought of the eggs not hatching. He searches the horizon for a ship or a smudge of smoke or the top of a distant mountain. But there's nothing. The bath is becalmed.

Words from a poem flit through his mind.

*Day after day, day after day,*
*We stuck, nor breath nor motion*
*As idle as a painted ship*
*Upon a painted ocean.*

He shares the birdseed with the finches, eating only a small amount for himself. In the heat of the sun he stretches out naked beneath the coffee table. He starts to grow weak. All he can think about is finding something for the birds to make into a nest.

He falls asleep with his head resting against the bars of the cage. Then he's startled awake by a little pricking sensation on his head. Then another and another, one after the other. The birds are pecking out his hair.

The boy sits up and pats his head. Then he bends over and places his skull even closer to the bars. The birds peck some more. All day the birds pull out the boy's hair. One hair at a time. It is painful but he lets them pluck away like crazy. Day after day.

Hour after hour. Minute after minute. Second after second. They pluck and pluck and pluck.

A week passes. By this time the boy is totally bald and becoming delirious. The birds have pulled out every hair. And they have built a lovely nest out of it. The female lays four eggs and takes turns with her mate to sit on the eggs.

Finally the seed runs out. The wind gets up. Salt water starts to slop into the bath.

A voice says, 'Hello there.'

The boy looks up. He is saved. Fishermen take him on board their boat and deliver him and the birds back to his mother who is overjoyed to see her son and does not tell him off even once. When the baby birds are fully grown he takes them all into the mountains and releases them.

And even though his hair never grows back, the boy is happy. He grows up to be a forest ranger who protects all the birds that fly free in the air.

# THE NEST

## 6

The door flies open and a figure falling into the room amongst gusts of howling wind and a flurry of snow and sleet shocks me awake. A red blur rolls across the floor like a bundle falling off a truck. I race across the hut and fight the door back against the tempest. Then I turn.

'Charlie,' I shout.

She rises on her knees and I help her to her feet. She is totally soaked and shuddering uncontrollably. Her strength has been sucked out by the storm and I can see that she's only just made it to the refuge.

She can hardly move. She's gone into shock. Frantically I start to take off her wet clothes. I have to get her dry and warm – nothing else matters. I wrap her in a blanket and sit her on the sofa in front of the fire.

'Are you okay?' I say anxiously.

She doesn't have the energy to answer so I stoke the fire and wait. The best thing to do is let the heat of the fire and the blanket slowly warm her body and ease her mind. The flames light up the cabin walls with a million glowing sunsets. Neither of us speak as we surrender to the shelter's embrace.

When we are both calm I stand and search the cupboards where I find several more sets of thick clothing. Charlie whispers her thanks and I can see that she's recovering. I squat to one side of the fireplace and listen to the rustle of the dry clothes as she puts them on.

'Robin, come and sit next to me,' she says.

Now that she's safe and warm I do as she says.

'What are you *doing* here?' I ask.

'What are *you* doing here?'

She takes my hand. Hers is still cold and she speaks

in a soft, trembling voice. 'Oh, Robin, I'm so sorry. I read your letter today – Dad talked me into it.'

'Shhh,' I say. 'It's okay.'

But her words tumble out. 'I should have realised what was happening with the bird. It's typical of me to jump to conclusions. I only had half the story. When I finished reading I rushed out. I had to find you and tell you that I believe in you. I saw you go up the track and I followed. I should've known you had a reason for breaking that little bird's neck. You were ending its suffering.'

This is the Charlie I remember.

'So bad of me,' she says. 'You couldn't hurt a fly.'

I don't know if that's true but the real Charlie is here now, and I trust her. When the time comes I might be able to tell her about my father and my terri . . .

I gasp. 'Dad,' I yell. 'He might still be out there in the storm. He's been out all day. I have to go find him.'

How could I have forgotten? Selfish, selfish, selfish. He tells me this all the time and he's right. I fell asleep and forgot about him. I rush over to the fire and start to put on my parka which is now almost dry.

'What do you mean?' cries Charlie, startled. 'Where's your father?'

'He went birdwatching.'

'Birdwatching!' she cries. 'Him? Are you sure?'

'I'm sure. He told Don Baker. Near the mineshaft. That's where I was heading when the storm hit. He might be there.'

'Might be! He'd have gone home when he saw the bad weather coming in, wouldn't he? You can't go out in this blizzard!'

'I have to,' I shout. 'I'll never forgive myself if I just leave him to die.'

'Well, I'm coming too.'

'No you're not. You're exhausted and anyway, you have to stay here in case something goes wrong. If I don't return you'll have to wait out the storm and then go for help, otherwise we could all die.'

Charlie doesn't protest anymore. We both know that what I've said is true. We both know the rules. We've lived up here all our lives.

'Don't leave here until it's safe,' I say as I put on my skis.

I open the door and the wind hits me like a falling wall. I force my way out into the blinding storm and leave Charlie to fight the door closed from the inside. I am alone in the blizzard.

I trudge forward, mainly by guesswork, because visibility is only a few metres. I'll never find my father unless the storm abates.

As if in answer to a prayer, the wind drops, the sleet stops and snow begins to fall gently. Now I can see the track which is heading downhill. So far so good. I keep a lookout for the narrow turn-off to the mine.

There it is. And there's the Ski-Doo, already thick with snow. Dad must have left it here because the track to the mine is too narrow and rocky. The tight passage through the trees isn't suitable for skiing either, so I slip my feet out of the toeholds and lean the skis against the dead machine.

Each footstep sinks deep into the fresh snow as I make my way clumsily along the track. I hardly notice the scratching branches and handfuls of ice dropped on my shoulders by the drooping trees. At last I break into the clearing and see the boarded-up mineshaft. And a figure working furiously. He's just a black shadow but I know it's my father.

Now he's peering into the vertical shaft. Behind him is a pile of rotting boards and beside them I see the sharpened icepick and a coil of thin rope attached to its handle. He's ripped a hole in the middle of the timber covering the shaft.

Some instinct tells him to look up. For a second he blinks, wipes the snow from his glasses and stares like someone who's woken from a coma. 'Robin?' he says.

'What are you *doing*?' I say as I close the gap between us.

'Swallows,' he says, nodding at the black hole.

'What? You won't find them down there, Dad! Not at this time of year,' I say, thinking he's gone crazy too.

'No,' he says. 'Why have you come?'

'To find you! There was a blizzard. Why didn't you go to the refuge?'

'I know what I'm doing,' he says. 'I've got all the right gear. Where's yours? Whatever possessed you to come up here without a pack?'

His words remind me of my mission. I pull out the damp pathology report. 'What does this mean? Why did you have my DNA tested?'

He gives a coarse laugh. 'It's not yours, Robin.'

Oh, thank god. He *doesn't* know I'm crazy. But whose DNA is it?

'Does that mean you're not my father?'

He laughs even louder. 'No, you're my son, for my sins.' He reaches inside his parka and pulls out a thin plastic bag stuffed with straw. It's the nest.

'Has all this got something to do with Mum?' I cry.

'Mum,' he shouts. The word infuriates him. 'All these lonely years. She'd be here now if it wasn't for you. She left me . . . If only you'd never been born. You, you . . . It's all because of you.' He stands with his back to the hole.

Rage, rage, rage fills my head. He's *still* blaming me! Images flash, corks pop, snakes strike. His words turn the falling snowflakes black. My head is about to explode.

'What is? What's because of me?' I rush forward.

Then darkness falls over me like a gift from the devil.

When I come to, I'm lying on my side. I'm covered in several centimetres of powdery snow. There's no sign of my father. There are no tracks, no footprints, nothing. Nothing except the gaping black hole beside me which silently inhales the falling snowflakes.

I crawl to the edge and call out, 'Dad? Dad?'

A voice calls back. My heart thumps. He's still alive. I call again.

And hear myself. 'Dad . . . Dad . . . Dad . . .' My echo dies and leaves only silence.

It's finally happened – what I've always feared. I've done it. Killed my own father. Not with the icepick – it still lies on the pile of planks with the coiled-up rope, and there's no trace of blood on it. I must have pushed him to his death.

Maybe he's not dead. What if he's still alive? He

could be at the bottom of the shaft unconscious or unable to speak. Oh, what have I done? What can I do? I could go to get help but in my heart I know that he'll be frozen to death by the time I return. I stare into the void. There's no way I can lower myself down there. Even inside gloves my hands are numb and the rope's covered in ice. I'll just fall and then there'll be two bodies at the bottom of the shaft.

I know – I could try to snag a piece of his parka and pull him up.

I stagger to my feet, grab the icepick and thread it backwards through the thin rope, forming a giant hook. I lower it into the darkness. Soon there's only three or four metres left. What if I don't have enough? Just as this thought takes possession of me the line goes slack. The rope has reached the bottom. I jig it up and down.

My whole body is freezing and my back aches. Maybe he's *not* there. This dim ray of hope illuminates my despair but only for a second.

The line resists my pull. I've snagged something.

Shit, it's heavy. I pull on the rope with shaking arms. Cold sweat trickles down my forehead stinging my eyes. Whatever I've hooked is stuck fast. I heave again and there's movement. Finally I take in about half a metre of rope but it's too much for me. There's no way I'll get my burden to the top. Suddenly the line lets go and I fall over backwards and splat into the wet snow.

The line hasn't broken, though. I can still feel that the icepick is attached to something, but it's lighter – much lighter. I assess the weight like an angler working out the size of a struggling fish and then start to pull frantically, squinting down into the hole, trying to make sense of the blurred shape that's coming towards me.

There it is.

It can't be.

It's not.

Oh, hell.

I hold up the rope and see my worst nightmare dangling from the end. I've pulled up the hand of my father and it's swinging on the end of the line right in front of my face. The sharp end of the icepick has pierced his wrist and pulled the hand totally away from the arm. Oh, god.

Like an ancient fragment from a marble statue, my father's snow-covered hand points at me. He always said it was all my fault. This is his final but lasting accusation. I'll never be free from him.

This spectre rising from the bowels of the earth has returned to confront me and I know beyond doubt that I'm a killer. I shudder and the movement shakes the line. A glove of fresh snow falls from the hand. The icepick swivels slightly. The hand from hell now points over my shoulder. Time freezes.

I am not alone.

The hand isn't pointing at me . . . It points to . . . I turn with a gasp and see . . . and see . . . I can't take it in. Alive and panting is . . . my father! He holds the emergency pack from the bogged snowmobile. His face is contorted with fear. I didn't kill him. I didn't. Oh, thank god.

We both stare at the swinging hand. Some of the bones of the fingers are cemented with ice. There's no skin. The hand must have been in the shaft for years. I hold it up like a fisherman displaying his catch. My father's eyes move ever so slightly and begin to follow the hand which seems to beat time like the pendulum of a clock. Finally it's almost still except for a slow swivelling motion. He's transfixed. He drops the pack and gives a strangled cry as he staggers to the left. He runs to the right and again the hand swivels. The hand seems to follow him. He bends low as if under fire from a sniper and darts at an angle towards the shaft. He turns and shrieks as he sees that the hand has followed his flight.

'No, Miranda,' he shrieks.

Miranda. My mother! It's *her* hand that I have pulled up from the pit. She's dead and I'm holding up part of her body on the end of the line! I belch up despairing groans. For a moment all I can do is submit to these spasms of grief and rage. Finally I manage to choke out a few words.

'You killed her.'

My father is still mesmerised by the hand. He's terrified of its accusing silence. He suddenly takes a little backward run like a footballer lining up for a free kick and staggers over the pit. For a second he seems to be walking on air. He disappears into the hole with a scream. The swirling snowflakes follow him like tiny petals thrown into a grave. I stand a numb and frozen mourner at the edge.

A choking sound erupts. Is it from him? Or from me? I can no longer tell what's real and what's not and for an eternity there's nothing. But then I hear moaning and the sound of rocks falling. I want to peer into the hole but I can't.

I hear my father scrabbling for purchase on the frozen edge of the pit. His head emerges, glistening and wet.

'Help me,' he gurgles. 'Please help me.' He sees the icepick. 'No,' he screams. 'No, no, no.'

I swing the line towards me and gasp as the bones of my mother's hand fall in a shower, disappearing into the snow. Images of death pop into my consciousness. I grab the handle of the icepick, raise the needle-sharp point and . . .

. . . extend it to the helpless, hopeless man. He clutches the handle and I pull with all my strength. He's too heavy. I can't hold on for even a few seconds more. He's going to fall. The handle of the icepick is slipping through his fingers. He's going to die.

A red arm reaches past me to take some of the load. 'I've got him too,' says Charlie. 'We can do this.'

'Charlie, you're here . . .'

Slowly we drag the desperate man out of the pit and collapse onto the snow. I roll over and stare into the abyss.

It is dark down there.

My father is an inert lump, wet and incoherent as he lies close to the mineshaft on his back with closed eyes.

'We have to get him moving,' Charlie says. 'He could freeze to death otherwise.'

We grab one arm each and more or less drag the pathetic figure along the rocky track to the Ski-Doo. We lay my father to one side while we sweep off as much snow as we can, then help him on to the machine behind me. Charlie climbs onto the rear seat herself and holds him in place while I start the cold engine. I let out the clutch too quickly, sending the groggy passenger lurching to one side. Charlie just manages to prevent him dropping onto the icy snow.

'We'll never get him home,' she shouts.

'You're right.'

I turn the snowmobile back uphill to head for the shelter of the storm refuge. The snow begins to swirl around our heads again – we're in for another heavy fall. I increase speed as much as I dare and we bump along as the wind whistles and drives the snow in gusts into our faces. The buzz of the motor is only just audible above the sounds of the weather.

Finally we reach the hut. My father awakes from his shivering coma, wipes his glasses and shakes his head furiously. 'I'm not going in there,' he yells.

What? What's the matter with him? He must know we can't possibly get home in this weather. 'Don't be stupid,' I say as I switch off the motor.

Charlie and I grasp an arm each and start to lead him to the door but he resists like a dog being dragged to its death. He seems terrified of the place.

'Alan, it's safe inside,' says Charlie.

'No,' he screams.

'Yes,' I say. He makes one desperate attempt to shrug us off and then slumps, slack and defeated, and allows us to lead him into the refuge.

We take off his outer clothes and the warmth of the fire which is still smouldering immediately begins to revive him. He peers around with a wild expression as if looking for ghosts that might somehow appear out of the walls and carry him off. Then, in an instant, he shrugs off his fear and walks straight to the closed cupboard where the emergency clothing is stored.

I try to help him with his wet clothes but he pushes me off. 'I can do it.'

This is a relief because the thought of touching him revolts me. 'Suit yourself,' I say.

Charlie and I sit on the sofa holding hands. 'What's going on, Robin?' she says.

My father hears her, even though the storm is howling outside. 'He's got it all wrong,' he chokes out. 'I know what he thinks . . .'

'It's not about thinking,' I yell. 'It's about the tru–'

Charlie then squeezes my hand so tightly that my knuckles bunch together. She whispers loudly. 'Let him speak. There're always two sides to a story.'

'Not with him, there's not,' snarls my father. 'He's never given me the benefit of the doubt. He only thinks the worst.'

'Now I see you as you really are,' I say. 'I'm not making any more excuses for you.'

'Ungrateful brat!'

'Murderer.'

Charlie gasps at the word. 'Robin!' she exclaims.

His response is accusing and hard. 'I didn't kill her. I've only known for sure that her body was up here somewhere since I got . . .'

'Body?' yelps Charlie, jumping up from the sofa. 'What body?'

'My mother's body is down the mine,' I say. '*He* put it there. He was trying to get her out when I found him.'

'No,' he says. 'You're wrong. She must have fallen in.'

My stomach starts to spasm again as the enormity of what happened at the mineshaft threatens to kill all rational thought.

'You *killed* her,' I spit out, standing up too. '*And* you've been here before. You knew where the fresh clothes were.'

'You're smart, aren't you, but you know nothing.'

'How did you know where her body was if you didn't do it?'

'Stop it, stop it,' cries Charlie, her hands over her ears.

At this point my father retreats into himself and moves closer to the fire, squatting down in front of it, claiming the warmth for himself as usual. His back is turned to us which doesn't surprise me one bit. He suddenly stands, walks to one of the bunks, lies down and pulls the blankets up over his head.

It's like he's closed the door, leaving us outside. He's not going to explain himself – not to me, anyway.

Charlie whispers again, soft but urgent. 'Robin, this is terrible. What's going on? It's madness. You're both scaring me.' She starts crying then and I put my arm around her. I lead her back to the sofa and we snuggle up by the fire, staring into the flames.

After a short time my father's breathing becomes regular and I know he's asleep. It's amazing that he can shut down like that and I'm glad he has. Charlie and I are alone. I tell her everything.

Almost.

It was a hot summer's day in inner-city Melbourne. Don Baker stepped down from the witness box after confirming that he'd seen my father on the mountain near the place my mother's body was found. Don had told him that swallows had been nesting in the old mine for years and he'd seen my father head off in that direction.

Having satisfied himself about that, the coroner recalled my father to the stand where he sat with a defensive, self-pitying face. I had to force myself to look at him as he squirmed under the questioning. In the past I'd told myself he didn't really mean the terrible things he'd say to me. Either that or I'd excuse his abuse, feeling sorry for him because he'd had a hard life. But now I could see that he was obsessed with one thing: himself.

'So tell me, why did you run off to the refuge with your baby son?' the coroner asked. He was trying to keep his tone neutral but it was obvious he had a low opinion of the man in the box.

'My wife had written a note. I found it on her dressing-table with her ring and hairbrush. She was planning to take Robin and leave me. I had to stop her. After all I'd done for her, she was just going to clear off without a word.'

'So you took the baby and skied up to the refuge because you knew she wouldn't leave without him?'

'Yes.'

'How long did you think you could hide up there? How did you plan to look after the baby?'

'I took supplies. I knew there were provisions in the hut and I took a backpack with baby food and formula and other stuff for Robin.'

'You must have known that his mother would follow you?'

'No,' he replied, fixing his eyes at a point in front of him.

'Wouldn't she have followed your tracks?'

'It was snowing. Pelting down. My tracks would've been covered in no time and I didn't think for one moment that she could have found us. She was unpredictable. You never knew *what* she would do.'

'Go on,' said the coroner.

'The weather closed in. I only just made it to the hut when the full storm hit. I was snowed in with Robin for a week. When I returned, Miranda was gone. I figured she'd run off with another man.'

'When in fact she'd gone looking for you and Robin and fallen to her death.'

'Yes,' agreed my father. 'She can't have known the mineshaft was there and must have walked over the rotting boards which would have been buried under the snow.'

'You took her baby in order to stop her leaving you?'

'I already told you that. He was my son too.'

Not anymore, old man, I thought. Not anymore.

The coroner hardened his tone. 'So you abducted him? Weren't you aware that's an offence in this country?'

'Well, she was going to take him from *me*.'

'But *she* left a note saying she'd contact you. You left her no idea where her child was at all.'

'Miranda wasn't fit to bring up a child. She had outbursts of temper. She was a liar and . . .'

He stopped short. I wanted to shout out '*you* are the liar', but I kept quiet. There were no words that could express my grief. There was no hurt I could inflict on him that would compensate for the loss of my mother.

I pushed these images aside as the coroner continued. 'So we come to the present. How did you know that your wife's body was in the mine?'

The court was hushed. I looked around at some familiar faces. Mrs Baker, Bazza, Mr Rogers, and Russell and Louise.

'It was the DNA,' my father was saying. 'I took a

sample of her hair from the brush in Robin's room and a sample from the . . .'

I already knew the rest. I couldn't take any more of him. I rushed out into the bright light of day. Trams clattered along the streets next to footpaths filled with hurrying people intent on agendas of their own. It *had* been a hell of a long season with the snow lasting until late September, but summer always comes in the end. I could just make out the distant ranges shimmering blue through the heat haze. Charlie followed me out and put an arm around my waist. We both stood in silence and let the sunshine drain away the anger.

It was nearly autumn before we were able to get Mum's remains from the Coroner's Court. We held the funeral at White Mountain Cemetery not far from where she died. The scented bush made a wonderful chapel and the birds sang the only hymns that were needed. I wanted the burial to be private – Mum had no other relatives but me. My father, wisely, decided not to attend.

I wrote a few words for the occasion, which I read to the small group consisting of Russell, Louise, Charlie, Grandpa, Moose, and Mary and Don Baker. I didn't want anyone from the school. The two funeral directors stood discretely in the shade of some snow gums.

It was only a small tribute, not my best writing really, but it came from the heart. I choked back tears as I read it aloud:

*Dear Mum,*

*I can't remember you but I know that you loved me and that it was enough love to fill the empty places which have opened up inside me from time to time. Sometimes I feel a harshness inside myself but it is always extinguished when I think of you. I have seen your face on the frozen windowpane and in the clouds and felt your presence carried on a gentle breeze and a flurry of snow. I know that you gave your life looking for me and that there is no love like . . .*

At this point I could feel my voice begin to give up the fight to hold an even tone. I stopped and gestured to the two men in grey. They quietly stepped forward to lower the coffin into the mountain soil. As my mother began her last journey I walked forward and placed my tribute on the polished wood. Not flowers, but the nest into which the swallows had woven strands of her long red hair.

My father wasn't charged with any crime. He moved to Queensland and I haven't heard from him since. I'll probably contact him one day even though he doesn't want to see me. He's only human and we all have our demons. I should know: I've got enough of my own.

It turns out that the workshop and lodge were left to me in my mother's will. So I no longer repair snow-mobiles for the Mountain Rescue Service or Integrity. I've leased the workshop to a cross-country hiking and skiing outfit which enables me to stay at school and finish my studies. I'm in Year Eleven now and doing well in English and Literature. I hope to go to Melbourne Uni.

Verushka and Ryan got back together again – I guess the way she used me to make him jealous worked – but it didn't last for long. The rumour is that she borrowed quite a bit of money from him and then took it with her when she left the mountain like she'd always wanted to. No one knows where she is now, not even him.

The warm weather lingers on well into April. Charlie and I are climbing up a narrow trail that winds steeply through Finnegan's Forest. The trees reach up to the sun, releasing a heady eucalyptus fragrance. Bellbirds squeak all around us and the last wildflowers peek out from rocky nooks. The mossy green and white of winter has given way to a dry carpet of fallen bark and branches. Autumn leaves crackle underfoot.

From time to time I stamp loudly on the baked surface of the winding track.

'You're not frightened of snakes, are you?' laughs Charlie.

'Isn't everyone?'

'They'd hear you coming and get out of your way. You're a lot bigger than them.'

'They're unpredictable,' I say.

We break into the open where a clump of boulders rests like giant marbles. 'Let's sit down,' suggests Charlie.

'Okay,' I say.

We sit for a while looking at the scarred cliffs which fall dizzily into the patchwork quilt of the valleys and lower slopes of the mountain range. Our bodies are touching and I can feel the electricity flowing between us. Charlie gives me a smile and begins to unbutton her shirt. It's not until she reaches the third button that I realise what she's doing. I can't believe her boldness. And generosity – risking herself with me in this way. I'm blown away with wonder and happiness unlike anything I've ever imagined or thought possible.

'I love you, Robin,' she says. Her eyes are so trusting.

I gently take away her hand and do up the buttons.

Her head jerks back as if I've slapped her. 'What's wrong?' She leaps up from where we're sitting and straightens her top.

'Charlie, please sit down. I need you to understand. I have to tell you something about me. You have to know what you're getting into before we go any further.'

'Why should I?' she says in a voice made of lead. 'This is the second time you've done this to me.'

'I didn't mean to hurt you,' I say. 'What you're doing is the most wonderful thing that's ever happened to me.' I swallow hard. 'Listen, it's this: I've got a terrible problem which I've never mentioned to anyone.'

She's concerned now. 'What do you mean?'

'I started to tell you that day in the forest, just before

I saw that little bird suffering and you ran off.'

'You mean there's more? Not just what you told me in the letter?'

'Yes, there's more . . . I want to tell you . . .'

I can't go on. What will she think of me when she learns the truth?

Charlie hesitates, then . . . 'It's okay, Robin. Don't bottle it up. You can tell me.'

So I do. I begin to talk, not looking at her, telling her about the dreadful pain caused by the glimpses of hell which have been inexplicably flickering into my mind without warning for about three years. I let it all pour out, not hiding anything, until there's nothing left to say. I feel completely drained.

Charlie remains silent.

I've done it now. I've lost her.

But she looks into my eyes again and says, 'Robin, it's okay. We can work this one out.'

'We can? You'll help me?'

'Robin, you told Mr Rogers that you didn't have anything to tell him, but you do.'

'Steve?' I say.

'Yes.'

'Okay, I'll go and see him.'

A blue wren flits happily nearby, pecking at the ground.

Charlie takes my face in her hands and pulls it towards her own. She kisses me gently on the lips. It is so good.

Oh, yes.

# The Snake

And they all lived happily ever after? Not really, not if you think about it. Take the story of the Frog Prince.

A beautiful princess came along and took pity on a poor ugly frog. She kissed him without knowing that he was really the king's son and he turned back into a handsome prince. They were married and lived a life of peace and joy for the rest of their days.

That's how it happened in the fairytale but in real life, after they were married, the prince would sometimes get out of his bed in the middle of the night and sneak back to the pond and be a frog again for a while. He would get down there in the mud and sludge and eat flies and jump around and croak and call to the other frogs and do all the horrible things that frogs do. The princess could tell that he had been visiting dark and grubby places because when he came back she would see he was a bit muddy but she learned to live with it. And sometimes when she was grumpy over nothing at all, the prince would pretend not to notice and give her breakfast in bed to cheer her up. That's how it goes in real life: everyone gets down in the mud sometimes.

Take Gordon, for example.

He loved to wander in the forest but the thick and tangled trees were full of snakes of which he was terrified. There were black snakes and brown snakes and tiger snakes and many others besides. He was especially frightened of the tiger snakes because he knew that the females would chase anyone who came between them and their young.

One day Gordon was walking in the darkest part of the forest when he came to the bank of a wide river. He sat down and stared into the gently flowing water, lost in thought. So deep was his reverie that at first he failed to notice an incredible change happening to his body. He reached down to pick up a stone to skim across the surface of the river and found that his fist was clenched tight and he couldn't open it. To his horror he saw the skin creep over his fingers. In no time at all there was only a large bulge on the end of his arm where once his hand had been. Two little buds began to grow on the knob; they quivered then blinked and opened. A pair of narrow, green, malevolent eyes met his. Gordon's hand had turned into a head which at that very moment was growing a mouth and fangs.

By now Gordon was almost crying with fear. But there was worse to come. A forked tongue appeared between the curved fangs and flickered in and out, mercilessly feeling for prey. Gordon no longer had fingers, no longer had a hand – instead he had his own snake and it was on the hunt.

'Aagh,' he screamed as the snake began to grow. Soon it was as long as two arms joined together. It curled and writhed. Its eyes were cold and cruel. Even though the snake was part of himself, or perhaps *because* it was part of himself, Gordon was terrified.

The snake hissed and felt for his face with its forked tongue.

'Don't,' screamed Gordon. 'Leave me alone.' The snake elongated its head like a stretched poma spring. Gordon struck first. With lightning speed he grabbed the snake behind its head with his left hand. The snake was angry and slippery and strong. Gordon fell to the ground, rolling and struggling to hold the terrible creature. It hissed as it sought him with wide open jaws. Two needle-sharp fangs each held a tiny drop of green poison.

'Stop it,' screamed Gordon. 'Go away. Leave me alone.' But the forest was empty. He wanted to run away but there was nowhere to hide from a snake that was part of himself. He could feel his left hand grow weaker as the reptile's cruel fangs reached for his eyes, his lips, his ears – any soft or vulnerable spot.

By now Gordon was exhausted and almost beaten by terror. His only weapon was his mind. Think, think, think. Do not surrender to this fate. Gordon grasped at a slender chance. Desperately holding the horrible head only centimetres from his cheek, he struggled to his feet and began to run towards the gently flowing river. With a warrior's cry of rage he leapt into the stream, landing on his feet in water up to his waist. With his left hand he forced the snake's head beneath the surface. It writhed and squirmed and struggled furiously.

Just when he thought he had won, Gordon felt his feet slipping. In a flash the tables were turned and he began to choke and breathe in water as his head sank beneath the surface. He staggered blindly to his feet, losing his grip on the snake which whipped back to make its final attack. Gordon punched the snake in the mouth, snapping off one fang with his knuckle, leaving the snake with only one curved tooth, still deadly – as dangerous as a sharpened icepick.

Before the snake could strike, a saviour arrived. A body floating gently towards them: a sleeping woman, as beautiful as a queen, carried by the current. Her eyes were closed but she smiled as if held in a magic dream. Her trailing dress flowed and rippled behind. Her long hair burned red in the sunlight. The snake was distracted. And attracted. The sleeping woman was better prey.

'No,' screamed Gordon. 'No. Leave her. Bite me! Bite me!'

The snake, infuriated by this selfless cry, turned his attention back to Gordon and granted his wish. It struck like a whip with its single tooth, biting the poor boy on the tongue. Gordon choked and fell back onto the bank as his tongue began to swell. Helplessly he surrendered to his fate. The snake twisted and turned, its tongue flickering in frustration at the sight of the sleeping woman floating away in the arms of the river.

To Gordon, the world seemed black and far away. His last thoughts were about the life the snake was stealing. This wretched reptile, this part of himself, was a filthy robber. From some unknown place he found the will to fight again and fumbled blindly at the forest floor with his good hand. A stick or a rock would have helped but there was nothing to grasp.

'Have some of your own medicine,' gasped Gordon. He opened

his mouth and chomped with his teeth. He bit the snake just behind the head. He bit down with the power of desperation. He bit with the will to live. He bit until the snake's bones broke and its green eyes turned red. He bit until its tooth decayed. He bit until the snake became what it had always been – an arm, a normal part of himself. He stretched his fingers. Oh, it was so good to have them back.

Gordon ran out of the enchanted forest and never returned. Later he met a beautiful princess, married her and lived happily ever after.

No he didn't. Sometimes, when the bloody moon is brooding, he creeps back to that place of snakes and birds and devils. That place of mud and madness and magic. After the kiss of a princess the frog pond will still call to him. And he must walk in the night for a while, for without the dark there is no day, nor star to see, nor tale to tell . . . to show the way.

*Robin Gordon, 2009*

ALSO BY PAUL JENNINGS

*How Hedley Hopkins Did a Dare . . .*

The UN series. Ten volumes

The Gizmo series. Four volumes

*Wicked!* With Morris Gleitzman

*Deadly!* With Morris Gleitzman

*The Reading Bug . . .*
*and how you can help your child catch it*

The Rascal series

*Round the Twist*

The Cabbage Patch series

The Singenpoo series

More information about Paul Jennings and *The Nest* can be found at
pauljennings.com.au and penguin.com.au/nest